JanIus: Platirius vs JanIus
Book III
D.L. Hannah

ISBN 9781965798225 2025

Contents

Isis, this is our third series! Let's get some ice cream!

Chapter 1

General Lyric entered Queen Vivant's bed chamber and found her bed empty. Assuming she was bathing, she turned to leave and spied her sitting on a balcony, her legs spread wide like a MaleForm's.

"Your Majesty?!"

Not recognizing the voice, King Anemi looked out of the corner of his eye and scowled.

Which of Queen Vivant's little wenches is this?

Being careful to mask his emotions, he slowly turned around and pasted on what he hoped was a welcoming smile.

"Yes?"

General Lyric's eyes bulged. "My Queen, you're not wearing undergarments."

"This thing gets hot!" he exclaimed.

Looking down at his crotch, he said, "I suppose I should shave it. What do you think?"

At the general's shocked stare, he said, "I guess not," and whirled around to take a short leap from the balcony.

General Lyric watched the queen stride like a MaleForm to her drawers and don a pair of silk panties.

Sitting on the bed, he awkwardly tried to cross his legs like a WomanForm. He supposed if she had permission to enter the queen's bed chamber at such an ungodly hour, it meant she was one of her trusted staff.

"What did you need to see me this early about?"

"I've been trying to access files about my mother. I've followed the proper procedures, but the system won't let me override the passcode. You're the only one with clearance to get in."

She paused. "I know I'm asking a lot, My Queen. It seems no one liked my mother, but I have to know what happened to her. Could you please access the files for me?"

Who the hell is her mother? he thought.

"I don't believe I met your mother," he said smoothly. "She died after I...came to Platirius to live with my father. What did you say her name was?"

"Lady Alarah."

He struggled to match a face to the name and came up empty. None of his former subjects had that name. Could she have been a...?

"A Coldarian?" he asked.

"Yes! She was born on Coldarius."

He frowned. "Then I don't see how I can help you. Coldarius's Hall of Records is gone."

"Yes, but she was living on Platirius when she disappeared."

Only my son would be stupid enough to marry a Coldarian and have the stench of them soiling up my kingdom.

"Ah, then I'll see what I can do—" A name flashed across his mind. "General Lyric," he finished.

"Yes, Your Highness. I can't thank you enough."

"Yes, well. That's what I'm here for—to help."

She bowed to him. "I'll round up the horses. The princesses are going riding this afternoon."

He had to be careful to conduct himself accordingly with Queen Vivant's daughters or they'd become suspicious.

"Watch over them carefully, Lyric. They're all I have."

"Of course, Your Majesty. You can count on me."

His smile faded once she left the chamber. She didn't see his silver eyes turn as black as a raven's.

"I have more important things to do with my time than research missing Coldarian whores," he said bitterly.

Sitting down at a small desk, he pulled up a list of all the Beings that had registered as citizens on Platirius on the TranScreen.

He paused when the photo of an attractive WomanForm appeared.

"Lady Alarah," he whispered. "You have an interesting face. But I don't need the Hall of Records to tell me what I want to know."

Summoning a spell, he catapulted himself back in time. A large soldier was viciously beating a WomanForm in front of King Dubian and Queen Opal. After hearing her broken confession, he smiled.

"So that's it. You betrayed Coldarius and allowed my idiot son access to King Carlomon's palace."

3

He watched her get tossed inside the Flames of Justice. *She's still there*, he thought.

He thought of how to use the newly found information against General Lyric on his way to the bath chamber. If he had to wear another of the queen's unbearably hot dresses, he'd shoot someone.

But if he wore trousers, someone might get suspicious. Donning a pastel blue day gown, he fashioned his hair into a messy bun and set out for the Flames. He nearly cursed when a lock of it fell out of place.

"Mother?" asked Princess Teenah, staring at Queen Vivant's hair. "What did you do to your hair?"

Princess Tyre snickered. "More like what haven't you done to it?" she retorted.

"I–I hurt my hand," he lied. "I'm not able to style it properly. Would you mind assisting me?"

Princess Teenah giggled. "Of course!"

He sat painfully through thirty minutes of Princess Teenah winding his hair into a style he was confident was reserved for prudes.

You certainly are a prim, boring fish, aren't you, granddaughter? Nothing like that flashy sister of yours.

Princess Teenah stood back, admiring her work. "How's that, Mother? I think you look beautiful!"

Smiling falsely, he pretended to preen in the mirror. "You did wonderful, my darling! You're so talented."

The princess smiled at him. "Thank you!"

"You're welcome. The general tells me you're going horse riding. Be careful and come back in time for luncheon."

"The general?" echoed Princess Tyre. "Mother, when have you ever referred to General Lyric as that?"

"I meant no harm," he said quickly. "I'm just so proud of her. I can hardly believe we have a female general now. It's so wonderful not to have MaleForms controlling everything, isn't it?"

The princesses looked at each other in confusion. Platirius had been under her reign for many years. They reminded themselves their mother had been through a lot, including being duped into believing they were dead. Perhaps what she needed was a long rest.

"You could say that again," said Princess Tyre. "Even though King Justin is running JanIus, he's doing a great job. Much better than if he were here."

His eyes darkened. "Why do you say that?"

"Well...the old kings would try to get inside his head. Everything you've built would be destroyed, and the WomenForms would go back to being miserable."

As you deserve, he thought.

His hand was balled up so tightly, his nails dug into his flesh. Checking himself, he unclenched his fist and patted her shoulder, careful not to break it as he wanted.

"Such smart young WomenForms. You make me so proud," he lied.

He nearly flinched when the princesses landed kisses on his cheeks.

"You make us proud too, Mother," said Princess Teenah. "In a while!"

"In a while!" said King Anemi. He waited until he was sure he was alone. "They even talk like Coldarians," he muttered. "Will I ever be rid of you, King Carlomon? I curse Dubian for marrying your wretched daughter."

The enchanting Flames rose high above the hills, almost touching Space. They walked slowly in front of the thousands of souls suffering within them. Their hands stretched out, desperately begging for mercy.

Ignoring their cries for help, they found Lady Alarah rocking back and forth on her knees. She was chanting an old Coldarian war song. It pleased them to see the Flames had driven her out of her mind.

"Rise, Lady Alarah, and face me."

She slowly looked up at them and frowned. "Who are you?"

"Stand, WomanForm. I don't answer to you."

They moved closer to the Flames.

"Would you like me to ease your suffering?"

She nodded furiously. "Yes, please. Please quench the fire. It's unbearable!"

Circling a hand before the Flames, they willed them to be still. Learning a young King Anemi had received a bit of the Flames as a reward for helping another sorcerer escape from hell had piqued their interest. After inheriting Platirius from his father, he'd used his magic to build the fiery prison to house souls, denying them access to The One's realm.

"I can release you. But...what will you do for me?"

"Anything," she panted. "Anything you want."

They smiled. "That's the correct answer."

King Anemi moved along the familiar path toward the Flames of Justice with a lighthearted step. He knew every inch of Platirius. It thrilled him to walk through its halls again.

The first thing on his list was getting rid of Queen Vivant's tacky décor and restoring the palace to its former glory. When the cool, crisp air grew uncomfortably warm, he smiled.

He was almost there. Eager to see the Coldarian, he quickened his pace. If he were seen near the Flames, no one would question it. Platirius's ruler needed no one's permission to explore its grounds.

Stretching out his hands, he willed the Flames to die down. After his son sent him to hell, the sorcerer he'd helped had returned to assist him in escaping his agonizing fate.

Satan, powerless to reclaim him, granted him free rein to wreak havoc on Beings—in and out of the galaxy. Siphoning the energy of numerous hosts had kept him alive.

Once their bodies expired, he quickly found another unsuspecting victim. Now he was inside The One's Protector. He knew The One wouldn't destroy her—she was too valuable to Him. He chuckled at the irony and his good fortune.

Finally reaching where she was housed, he paused.

What's this?

She was gone!

I'm in Queen Vivant's vessel. Who else would release her? And why?

General Lyric rode with the princesses across the pasture. Willing her horse to go faster, she sped out into the open, her mind racing almost as fast as the horse.

"General Lyric!" cried Princess Teenah. "Please slow down, I can't go that fast!"

At the princess's request, she pulled on the reins, slowing her pace. They reached a small embankment closed off by a flowing stream.

Princess Teenah elevated her voice over the roaring sound of the waterfall. "Rubarius used to be over there. Now the palace is gone."

Princess Tyre took in the magnificent gardens and dozens of small ponds. "It's still beautiful."

"And cursed," muttered General Lyric.

As Princess Tarah's horse approached them, the general said, "Beauty can be deceptive. Sometimes it hides the darkest souls."

Princess Teenah looked at her. "Are you alright, General Lyric?"

Her violet-gray eyes remained on the land. "I'm fine. Let's get back to the palace. The queen is expecting a guest for dinner. We shouldn't be late."

Princess Teenah smiled. "I'll bet it's King Asa!"

Princess Tarah frowned. "Now, why would you say that? He hasn't been around since our last battle."

"No, because Mother visits him on Onzi!" said Princess Teenah. She giggled. "It's so romantic!"

Princess Tarah glared at her. "In whose eyes? He doesn't care about Mother. All he wants is to become Platirius's king. Then we'll go back to being under a MaleForm's control!"

"Mother wouldn't let that happen," said Princess Tyre. "She already promised us no MaleForm would rule Platirius, and I believe her! He may be good-looking, but the only place he'll rule is Onzi."

"I still don't like it! She's married to our father!"

"Aht! Aht!" said Princess Tyre. "Father has been gone for eighteen long years. Galactic law declares a Being dead after twelve. How long do you expect her to mourn for him?"

"Well, you seemed to have gotten over it pretty quickly!" snapped Princess Tarah.

"*None* of us remember him, Tarah! You speak as if he just died yesterday!"

"How do we know he's really dead?" asked Princess Tarah hotly.

"Oh, By The One," groaned Princess Tyre. "Not this again. Listen. You can sit and play detective if you want, but I say Mother is still young. She's allowed to have fun with a male companion if she wants to! She doesn't need you dragging up the dead every five seconds to shame her back into mourning!"

Princess Teenah looked nervously at her sisters. Having the sunniest personality of the trio, she often avoided conflict and drama.

"He was our father," said Princess Tarah. "Not some space hound that showed up at our doorstep and disappeared one day. How could you be so callous?"

Princess Tyre scowled at her. "And how can you walk around so miserable all the time? You're such a downer! No one can have any fun around you anymore. You changed after we were kidnapped and taken to Revani."

"That's right! I changed for the better and learned to take things seriously. We may be triplets, but we think differently. I don't go through life believing everything is a game!"

"That doesn't set you above the rest of us," said Princess Tyre evenly. "Becoming Aunt Reve's soldiers changed our perspectives on who we are and what our duty is to Platirius. I spent three years following orders. I think I'm allowed to kick my heels up and have fun if I choose to."

"Well, don't let me stop you," said Princess Tarah bitterly. "I choose to find out what really happened to our father!"

"Do you hear yourself?" asked Princess Tyre. "You sound like one of those Human detective shows. What really happened? He died in battle just as the records say. Alright, we never found a body. So what? Do you realize how many soldiers never come home from war?"

Princess Tyre turned her horse around. "If you want to live in the past, by all means, go ahead. But leave me out of it! General, I'm ready to return to Platirius when you are."

She took off without waiting for an answer. Princess Tarah watched her sister leave, shaking her head. "She doesn't care."

"I believe she does," says Princess Teenah. "We all care about Father, but what's done is done. And she's right about Mother. I want her to be happy. She deserves it. So do you, Tarah."

Slapping the reins against the horse, she sped off behind Princess Tyre, with Princess Tarah and General Lyric following close behind. A flash of anger shot through Princess Tarah.

I don't care what you say, Tyre. I'll get to the bottom of what happened to Father. With or without your help!

"I'll get that for you, My King!" said Captain Josin.

King Justin sighed. This was the third time he'd tried to move his belongings out of the cottage King Leighton had assigned to him.

"Captain Josin, I'm very capable of moving my own things."

Fawn appeared in the doorway and laughed. "You should get used to it, Your Highness. Being a king comes with perks."

"I don't mind the perks," he told her. "I just don't like feeling incompetent. Being waited on hand and foot isn't for me."

"I think it's too late for that, My King," she said.

He groaned. "Oh no. Not you too. Do you think you can return to calling me Justin?"

She shook her head. "No. And I'd better not see anyone else trying it." Her tone turned serious. "You are our king now. Things will never go back to how they were before King Leighton died."

King Justin lowered his head. "You mean before I killed him?"

She shrugged. "That's how things work here. This isn't Earth. Being a king isn't something you do for eight years, then return to your normal life. It's a lifetime appointment."

She tilted her head until he looked at her. "Yes, you ended his life, but with his blessing. Had you not, King Belial would've conquered JanIus and where would we all be?"

"This sounds like one of our old pep talks. No hand on the shoulder this time?"

"No. Only the loved ones of royal families are permitted to touch them. That is a silent and understood rule across the galaxy. It's the way of things."

"Maybe it shouldn't be," said King Justin.

She sighed. "I won't pretend to understand how you feel. You've been thrust into all of this in the blink of a star. Nevertheless, King Carlomon entrusted you to continue Coldarius's legacy through JanIus. Being a king isn't an easy task, but you wouldn't have been chosen if you weren't qualified."

The soldiers continued removing boxes from the bed chamber as they talked.

"One of your duties is ordering your soldiers to do whatever needs to be done. That includes me. If you start letting them drop your title and treat you like a friend or acquaintance, there goes your respect and your first line of defense. I wouldn't start anything you'd want to end. That's my humble opinion, Your Majesty."

"My aunt has an advisor. Maybe I need one too. Someone who can show me the ropes of how to do this king business the right way."

"I think that's an excellent idea, Your Highness."

"So do I," said Gallium. "You fight well with a BrainStaff, but you should know how to fight without one too. King Belial almost killed you with that side wound. Not knowing how to block moves like that is the quickest way to end your reign."

Shifting his gaze from Fawn to Gallium, he said, "Well, I have soldiers but no general. How would you like to be mine?"

Gallium's eyebrow raised. "I'm married, King Justin."

"To a general," said King Justin.

"A general who won't leave Revani," countered Gallium. "I won't live separately from her."

"I wouldn't ask you to do that. I saw the way you travel through space—like a shooting star. JanIus is peaceful—"

"For now," said Gallium.

"So you wouldn't need to stay here all the time. How about it, Gallium? I know my mother won't give you that level of rank in her army. I need you here. I think it's what my great-grandfather would've wanted."

A knock at the door interrupted them.

"You wanted to see me, King Justin?" asked Sergeant Lionus.

"Yes, Sergeant, I did. I wanted to tell you I was very impressed with your skills when we fought King Belial. I'd be thrilled to have you in my army."

"Whoa," said Sergeant Lionus. "I'd be honored, My King!"

He bowed to King Justin and said, "Never thought I'd live to see the day I'd be under King Carlomon's great-grandson!"

"Good," said King Justin. "Fawn, he'll need new uniforms. I haven't learned who's in charge of that yet."

"That would be Captain Josin, Your Highness. I'll find him and let him know."

"Thank you, Fawn."

Sergeant Lionus turned to Gallium. "Are you our general?"

"That's what I'd like to know," said King Justin. "I've already told him he's needed here."

14

"Let me talk it over with Legend," said Gallium. "I don't know how she'll take it, but to be honest, I've missed the camaraderie of MaleForms."

Sergeant Lionus grasped his shoulder. "It'll be like old times, General Barrios. Without King Dubian. Man, I would've given anything to see him die. I hear Queen Revari ended him."

"She did," said Gallium, smiling. "It was a glorious day."

Gallium and Sergeant Lionus laughed.

Sergeant Lionus's smile faded. "Oh, I'm sorry, Your Highness."

"For what? I have no love for him."

"Well, he's still your...family."

"If it weren't for General Legend, he would've murdered me in front of my mother. And he locked her away for years. You and I won't be cracking jokes about him, but I have no goodwill toward him."

The timekeeper chimed softly on the wall.

"It's about time for the troops to change shifts. I'm placing you on the day shift, Sergeant. If you have any questions or issues, please come and find me."

The sergeant bowed. "I will, My King. And thank you again."

As he turned to leave, King Justin said, "Oh, Sergeant?"

"Yes, Your Highness?"

"I want you to keep a close eye on Captain Josin. Watch everything he does, then report back to me—especially if you see anything suspicious."

The sergeant saluted him. "I'll take care of it, King Justin."

After he left, Gallium asked, "Is Josin the one who arrested you?"

"Yes."

"I trust Sergeant Lionus with my life. He respected King Carlomon. You won't find a more loyal soldier to your throne. You think this Josin is trouble?"

"I know he is," said Justin. "For a split second, I saw his face when I ended King Leighton. He has a huge problem with me. Now that I'm king, I intend to solve it for him."

Gallium cracked his knuckles. "That doesn't surprise me since I know your mother. You may look like your father, but you have her spirit. And King Carlomon's too. He was kind, but he didn't tolerate nonsense."

"I didn't plan on being a king, but Fawn is right. It's done now."

He thought of Ms. Dill and the triplets.

"I'm going to be a ruler my subjects can rely on. King Carlomon trusted me. I'll make him proud if it takes me the rest of my lifespan."

That earned a smile from Gallium.

"I think you've succeeded already, but what do I know? Now I'm going home to talk to my wife. I'll have an answer for you before luncheon."

"Thank you, Gallium. You know, it feels strange to say, but when you're around, I feel King Carlomon's presence. Nothing would make me happier than if you would join me."

Gallium placed a leather cap on his head. "It's nice to be wanted again."

"Hey, since when did you start wearing hats?"

"Since now!" he called over his shoulder. "In a while, My King!"

King Justin laughed. "In a while!"

F awn had just sat down to eat lunch in her office when she looked up and saw a visitor standing in the doorway. Thrown off guard, she quickly stood and bowed.

"Queen Revari! This is a surprise. Welcome to the Azini Institute." She looked over the queen's impeccable clothing. "Are you hurt?"

"My eyes are," said Queen Revari, taking a seat in front of her. "Every time I see General Lyric on my son's arm, I almost go blind."

Her eyes raked over Fawn's lab coat. "You may be seated, Dr. Azini."

"May I have one of the staff bring you a meal from the café down the street?" She nodded toward her takeout container. "They have excellent seafood and Cuban dishes."

The stunning queen calmly assessed her. "No, thank you. I didn't come here for food."

Fawn tried to fight down a wave of anxiety as Queen Revari scrutinized her office.

"You've done well for yourself. I suspected you would if given the right opportunities."

Examining one of Fawn's tall purple lemon trees, she said, "I have some things you might like in my palace. I'll have them shipped out to you."

"Than-thank you, Your Highness!" stammered Fawn.

Queen Revari set her expensive bag on Fawn's desk and folded her hands in her lap.

"Do you remember how you acquired all of this?"

"Yes, Your Majesty. It was through your generosity."

Queen Revari smiled. "You know, Dr. Azini, you're one of the few Beings I genuinely like. You've always shown proper respect—unlike my sister's detestable general."

"Thank you, My Queen. That's very kind of you."

General Revari's eyes narrowed. "Kindness has nothing to do with it. I gave you the life you've always wanted. Now I'm here to collect what you owe me."

"Name it, Your Majesty," said Fawn.

"Mother has a nice ring to it, don't you think? I don't have a daughter. Had my husband and I been left alone, maybe I would have. You could make that happen if you're smart."

Fawn blinked. "I...I don't know what you mean."

"You and my son. If you married him, you'd be JanIus's queen. Surely you want more than being a doctor?"

18

"Becoming a doctor is all I've ever wanted, Your Highness. King Justin enjoys my company, but I don't think he'll ever love me the way he loves General Lyric."

Queen Revari sucked her teeth. "That name! It's like nails on a TranScreen. I get so sick of hearing it. She's not polished like us. She's a commoner whose wicked mother had a hand in destroying my mother's planet. I'll die before I allow Lady Alarah's daughter to marry into my family."

Fawn pursed her lips. "Forgive me for asking, My Queen, but how will you stop it? King Justin sees the sun and moon in her eyes."

"Are you in love with my son?" asked the queen suddenly.

Fawn paused. The budding feelings she'd grown for King Justin were new and strange to her.

"I never thought it was possible to have feelings for a MaleForm, but he's kindhearted and sweet. He doesn't yell or threaten us if we make a mistake. He'd never raise his hand to a WomanForm either. I admire his patience and intellect."

"So do I," said Queen Revari. "He's grown to be someone his father would've been very proud of."

"I've kept my distance out of respect for his relationship. I have no intention of being the other WomanForm. Not that he'd go for it anyway. He's faithful too."

Queen Revari smirked. "But is she faithful to him? She's always put her career before him. Now she's become obsessed with finding out what happened to her decrepit MotherForm. She's convinced herself she was something she never was. A horse is a better mother than Lady Alarah was, but Lyric is so blind, she can't see it."

Fawn empathized with General Lyric. Her mother was toxic too. Content to drink her days and nights away, she'd grown addicted to sweet PotterBerry wine. She ate very little and had stopped helping with the chores. Fawn had been forced to hire cleaning staff.

She leaned forward and adjusted the collar of Fawn's smock. "A physician is a respectable profession, but being queen is everything. I want you to set your sights higher. With you by his side, my son will have a successful reign. Thanks to me, your graduation ceremony was one of the best times of your life. You do remember that night, don't you?"

Fawn did.

She'd been dispatched to report to the back of the instruction chamber, where her father and other doctors were waiting before the explosion. Two Revaltians led her to her father, who was lying on the floor, moaning in pain.

The blast had severed some of his limbs. She'd never forget the look on his face the last time she saw him.

"Fawn," he cried, reaching for her. "Fawn, please help me! Help me get out of here!"

Queen Revari looked down at him and smiled before turning to Fawn.

"Finish it," she said. "You know you want to."

Chapter 2

F inally, he was right where she wanted him to be—lying broken and helpless before her. She moved closer, taking in the damage the explosion had caused.

Witnessing the range of emotions dancing across her face, he said, "Fawn, I'm so sorry! If you help me, I'll let you work at my practice. I swear! Just—just help me get out of here!"

Filled with long-suppressed rage, emboldened by the opportunity to finally end him, she lifted her foot and brought it down on his neck. Unable to relieve himself of the pressure, he writhed and choked, desperately trying to get oxygen into his lungs. Fawn increased the weight on his throat.

His face turned a deep shade of violet. Desperate for air, he clawed at her foot. She snarled when his eyes bulged from his sockets.

"Die! Just die already!"

When the light finally drained out of his eyes, she felt no sadness or remorse. Instead, a huge weight lifted from her shoulders. She stepped back to survey him.

Pride rose within Queen Revari. "I see I've made an excellent choice! Do you want to harvest his organs, or shall I have him shipped into the sun as he is?"

"No, Your Majesty. No one should be cursed with any part of him."

"Very well," said Queen Revari. "Captain Cindy! Get a couple of soldiers to dispose of his body. Leave the rest for the emergency staff to take care of. You had a good ride, Fawn, but I hope you know none of this was free. One day I'll come to collect."

She left her standing over her father's corpse. Fawn wasn't bothered by the smoke circulating within the chamber. Breathing it deeply into her lungs, she exhaled and smiled. It smelled like victory.

The Present

"It's time to pay the piper," said Queen Revari. "I'm doing my part to break them up."

Fawn tried not to cower under the queen's intense scrutiny.

"And you, my little doctor, will finish the job. General Lyric will never become the queen of JanIus. Have I been heard?"

"Yes, Your Majesty. But what can I do? She's much prettier than I am."

The queen scoffed, waving her hand. "You give her far too much credit and don't give yourself enough. General Lyric has always looked and acted like a MaleForm. There's nothing feminine or demure about her."

She passed a small tube of lotion to Fawn. "My sister tried softening her up with makeup and clothes—but she's still just as gangly as a newborn chicken. There's a reason for that, Dr. Azini—shit can't be polished."

Admiring Fawn's curls, she said, "You have beautiful hair. Do something with it and stop wearing black, chaste clothes all the time. You're not in mourning. You're friends with the top fashion designer in the galaxy—Tese Blight. Use it to your advantage."

She glided silky smooth lip gloss over her lips before plucking one of the ripe lemons from the tree and stood. "I expect to see results. I have no doubt Lyric will trash what she has with him, and he'll need a soft place to land. You. He thinks very highly of you. So do I."

Moved by the compliment, Fawn stood and saluted her. "Thank you, Your Highness."

"Justin is a king now. I want him to have what I never did—a chance at a happy marriage, and to have beautiful babies. That's the dream I envision for him. I handed this life to you on a silver platter. Now it's time to return the favor."

Queen Revari strolled from her office as if she owned it. In fact, she did. And JanIus too. But her son didn't know that. If she had her way, he never would.

Queen Marietta sat in her dressing room, knitting a silk scarf for Queen Vivant. Since she'd married General Kron, she'd gifted one to her every year. Prince Jonah, her second son, waved his hand over the TeleShield and entered.

The scarf was balanced in the air in front of her, turning as she concentrated on perfecting the fine stitching.

"Mother? I don't mean to disturb you, but it's almost time. I don't think he has long."

The scarf halted just above her head. He kneeled in front of her, covering her hands with his.

"I remember when we first met," she said wistfully. "I was twenty summers and had just signed up for pilot training. My first class was to begin in a week. I took a TravelCraft back home. Or so I thought. I got into the wrong craft—a king's craft."

The scarf began turning again when she laughed. "His soldiers were fit to be tied. One pointed a finger in my face and told me I'd be marched in front of the justice council for trespassing. When he tried to escort me off the craft, your father entered."

Fascinated by her gift of telepathy, Prince Jonah watched her weave expensive thread into the scarf.

"I've never forgotten what he said: *Touch her and you'll answer to me.* I looked up and saw this broad-shouldered MaleForm with ginger hair and skin so bronzed, it looked like it had been kissed by the sun. His gray eyes sparkled like diamonds. My knees buckled like a young filly."

Moved by the great love his parents shared, he gently squeezed her hand.

"I was so scared, but he looked at me and said: *Nothing would bring me more pleasure than to have your company. Please allow me to take you wherever you're going.*"

When she broke concentration, the scarf fell into neat folds on her lap.

"I told him I was going home. He asked for the coordinates and told the pilot to take the long way back. We talked for over an hour. By the time the craft landed in front of my home, I was floating over the moon."

Her smile was as warm as the sun shining through the window.

"The next day, he invited my family for supper. After he asked my father for my hand, we were married six months later."

Her fingers lightly grazed the soft threads. "Lucian was born the following year. This is his favorite color—robin's egg blue."

Glancing at her wedding painting stirred nostalgia and longing within her. "Those were happy times. We've made so many joyful memories together."

Prince Jonah wished he could do something to ease her melancholy. "I think he's held on this long to see if we'd find Lucian, but his heart is giving out."

Her fingers ran rapidly through the scarf's thick, blue fringes. "He would give anything to see him again. So would I."

Prince Jonah sat next to her. "I've spoken with the family of Lucian's old pilot. They said before he died, he told them he was preparing for Lucian's flight just before he blacked out. When he woke up the next morning, he was at home and alone. But Lucian's craft was seen flying over Platirius on schedule. Now, if his pilot wasn't behind the controls, then who was?"

"I don't know, Jonah. King Dubian was so despised, his enemies hated Lucian too. Any one of them could've hurt him."

"But none of the other kings have admitted to harming him. Vivant said she was given a note claiming he'd been called to battle. No specifications were given, nor did she think to question it."

His hand balled into a fist. "I was a ChildForm when it happened. I was powerless to do something then, but not now. Someone set my brother up, and I'm going to get to the bottom of it."

Taking her hands, he stood, lifting her out of the chair. "Come, let us go to Father. He needs us now."

Queen Marietta laid the scarf over the arm of a chair. She'd lost her son, and now, her husband was dying.

"I can finish this later. Please alert Vivant and tell her to come. I know he'd want to see her and our granddaughters one last time."

Linking her arm into his, he said, "I'm eager to see them. I just wish it were under better circumstances."

"So do I, Jonah." She paused to look at herself as a young bride. "So do I."

"My Queen, there's an urgent message for you from Maieman," said Sergeant Alicia.

Irritated, King Anemi looked up from his chilled cucumber soup. This was the third time his meal had been interrupted.

Why hasn't Vivant taught these idiotic WomenForms to show proper respect to a ruler?!

"Is it important enough to interrupt my lunch?" he asked sharply.

Sergeant Alicia blinked, put off by the queen's sudden, abrupt tone. "Yes, Your Majesty. King Micah is dying."

Good! The insufferable prick.

Agitated, he stared at the sergeant. He couldn't care less if Maieman's king was dying, but if he said so, it might cause the queen's soldiers to get suspicious.

Masking his expression into a false show of concern, he said, "Have the surveillance team send the transmission to me."

The sergeant bowed. "Yes, My Queen."

Prince Jonah's face appeared on her TeleScreen.

"Hello, Vivant. I wish I were contacting you under better circumstances, but Father has taken a turn for the worse. Mother would like you and the princesses to come to Maieman and say goodbye."

Now why the hell should I go to Maieman for that?

"Of course, Jonah. You know how I feel about King Micah. How is Mother?"

"She's holding up. You know her—she puts on a brave front for everyone, but it's tearing her apart. Father has been ill for a while, but I don't think you ever get used to a loved one dying."

"That's certainly true," said King Anemi. "I'll take a craft first thing in the morning."

Prince Jonah shook his head. "I don't think he has that long, Vivant. It would be best if you came today. Mother needs you."

King Anemi held onto his temper. The gall of the Krons to summon him to Maieman like a commoner! For all he cared, King Micah could die and go straight to hell. But then...if he went, he'd get to see Marietta again. Gripping his spoon tightly, he ground his teeth.

She'd spurned his advances and married a king less powerful than him. To see her at her lowest point would be a feather in his cap. When he thought of it that way, a trip to Maieman seemed ideal.

"Very well, I'll gather my daughters. We'll head out within the hour."

Prince Jonah smiled. "Mother will be overjoyed to see you. In a while, Vivant."

"Wait, Jonah? When he dies, you'll be crowned king, yes?"

He paused. "Uh, well, of course."

He couldn't take his head. If Maieman were absorbed into Platirius, his cover would be blown. He smiled so hard at the prince, he nearly broke a tooth.

"I'm so happy for you, Jonah. I know how long you've waited for this day."

Prince Jonah blinked. "Vivant, I've never wanted my father to die!"

"I didn't mean it that way," he lied. "I meant you've taken such good care of your mother and your subjects. I'm sure they'll feel more at ease to see King Micah isn't suffering anymore. I understand you're under a lot of strain, but there's no need to snap at me."

"Vivant, I'd never snap at you. It's just an odd thing to say is all."

King Anemi cocked his head. "Oh? I don't believe there's anything wrong with what I said more than how you interpreted it. Since we all love Father, we should show each other respect at such a tragic time. Don't you agree?"

"Of course," he said. "I apologize. I meant no disrespect, sister. As you've stated, it's not the best of times."

King Anemi smiled. "Apology accepted, Jonah. Now, if there's nothing else, I need to prepare for the trip. We'll see you soon."

He disconnected the transmission, leaving Prince Jonah staring at the TeleScreen in shock.

"What in Maieman just happened?"

Shaking off the odd conversation, he hurried to inform the cleaning staff to prepare the east wing for guests.

After a sumptuous luncheon, King Anemi pushed away the dishes. The last place he wanted to be was Maieman. An alert buzzed inside his palm. He tapped his hand on his TeleScreen and waited for the message to transmit.

The doors of the military chamber flew open. Queen Opal stormed in with a half a dozen soldiers, her eyes blazing. King Anemi leaned forward, eager to watch the tense scene unfold.

"I'm going to give you one second to tell me the truth, or my niece will watch your carcass shipped off this planet in chains."

He blinked. "Your Highness?" Abruptly, he stood, looking at the soldiers behind her. "What is this about, Queen Opal?"

"You're going to tell me exactly why Coldarius was absorbed into Platirius. Don't leave anything out, General, or you'll die before my husband!"

He sank into his chair. "Send them out and I'll tell you everything I know."

Queen Opal sat down and picked up a sharp blade. "Start with everything about my husband's treachery. If you hurt my father, I'll see King Micah's throat slashed before dawn!"

Not only was his life on the line, his father's was too. He'd served under both sisters, each deadly and thorough to the bone. But Queen Opal had no conscience. That made her more lethal than Queen Dellah. He cleared his throat.

"On the night of his thirty-ninth LifeCelebration, he told me he wanted to get rid of Coldarius. He intended to bring a few of your family members, 50,000 soldiers, and 5,000 staff to work for him. He said...the rest would freeze to death on Coldarius."

Her hand tightened around the blade.

"He blackmailed me! He threatened to tell Princess Vivant I had a hand in Coldarius's demise if I betrayed him. I couldn't risk her finding out! I was scared. I didn't know what to do."

Frantically, he looked up at her, his eyes pleading for her to understand. Finding no trace of sympathy, the words fell out of his mouth like rocks tumbling over a cliff.

"I wanted to tell you so many times. But I couldn't betray him. He would've had my title stripped for treason." He rubbed his hand over his head in frustration. "And he would've had me killed."

Queen Opal pointed the blade at him. "This is exactly why ChildForms shouldn't be put in positions of power! You should've told my father the moment he revealed his plans! Now look what's happened. Coldarius and my father are gone. Everything I knew and loved has vanished!"

Drying her eyes, she said, "The only one who will die is Dubian. Tonight." She stood. "And you're going to help me do it."

"Yes, My Queen. But please...please don't tell my ParentForms! It would break them if they found out."

Her eerie demeanor informed him he wasn't in a position to ask for favors. Tossing the blade on the desk, she turned her back on him, leaving him sitting alone in the dark.

King Anemi laughed. "Ah! So your ParentForms don't know your nasty little secret, eh? It would...break their poor hearts," he said mockingly. "If King Micah isn't dead by the time I arrive, this will surely send him to his grave. And Marietta...I finally have the chance to pay you back for humiliating me when you married him."

He rubbed his hands together and said, "This will be a trip they'll never forget!"

Another call buzzed on the TeleScreen.

"Yes?"

"Hello, My Queen," said King Asa. "The week's end is approaching. I was wondering if I could fly you here to spend time with me?"

King Anemi scowled at him. "For what?"

Taken aback, he said, "We see each other every week. Have you grown tired of me?"

King Anemi's mind raced to discover what he meant.

Oh nooooo. I guess she's not a prude after all if she's been—

"I...I've been dispatched to Maieman. King Micah is dying."

King Asa's expression morphed from dumbfounded to one of empathy. "I heard he'd taken ill, but I'd hoped things would change. Vivant, I'm sorry. I know how close you are to your in-laws."

"Yes, well...everyone dies. I'm surprised The One dragged it out this long."

King Asa's eyebrow shot up.

"Anyway, I have to be there. It wouldn't look good if I skipped the DeathCeremony."

He flexed his broad shoulders. "He's not dead yet. There's still time for things to change."

I don't want them to. I want to see him choking on his last breath!

"You're right, King Asa. Well, I'd love to chat, but I have to get to Maieman. Goodbye!"

King Asa sat in his study long after the transmission had disconnected.

"Vivant has never forgotten our dates. She has a mind of steel!" He rubbed the coarse hairs of his beard. "Her mother reared her with Coldarian etiquette—she always says 'in a while,' never 'goodbye.' That's not something she'd toss aside. And since when does she address me as King Asa?"

He uploaded a photo of them taken on the night of the ParaNuture physicians' graduation ceremony on his palm. His hands were wrapped around her waist. The lovers smiled at each other as if they owned the universe. He sighed. That's exactly how she made him feel. Now she acted distant and formal.

"What in the galaxy is going on?"

Queen Revari entered Queen Vivant's bed chamber with a large bouquet of blue roses. Outside of the Amorous royal family, no one had access to them. Since Gallium had designed them for Queen Dellah, he refused to cultivate them for anyone except members of her family. She found her sister applying a pale pink lipstick. Eyeing the rose-colored hat and day gown, she whistled appreciatively.

"It's about time you started wearing brighter colors. What's the occasion, sister?"

King Anemi looked at her through the vanity's mirror. "How did you get in here?"

"I was once half of Platirius's ruler. Do you think any of your guards are high enough to stop me from entering it? And what's with the snarky tone?"

"King Micah is dying. I've been dispatched to Maieman. You remember him, don't you?"

"Yes," said Queen Revari, setting the roses on a small, but tall table. "He's General Kron's father. He spoke to me at your wedding."

Captain Thea entered. "My Queen, we've packed and loaded your belongings on your craft. The pilot is ready whenever you are."

"Good. You can go, Captain Thea."

Queen Vivant's dismissive tone and Queen Revari's raised eyebrow weren't lost on the captain, but she assumed the queen was upset about King Micah.

"You must really be upset," said Queen Revari. "I've never heard you speak to your soldiers that way before."

"That's because you didn't stick around long enough to see me under the full influence of Callidut," said King Anemi bitterly.

He held a diamond necklace under his chin. Queen Revari grabbed a set of pearls and draped them around his neck.

"Always wear pearls for DeathCeremonies. You taught me that. And Mother taught you. Don't you remember?"

King Anemi allowed her to fasten the rows of heavy pearls around his neck.

Damn. I need to be more careful around her.

"Yes. I guess I'm overwhelmed. King Micah has been ill for a long time, but I never expected I'd get the chance to see him die."

"Get the chance?" Queen Revari echoed. "I thought you loved him."

"I do," said King Anemi quickly. He covered his face with his hands, acting as if he were grief-stricken. "That came out wrong. I don't know what I'm saying."

"That's the wrong shade of lipstick."

He watched her skillfully remove it from his lips without smearing it.

Selecting a lipstick in deep mauve, she expertly applied it to his lips. Standing back to peruse her work, she said, "Your hair looks awful. Let's take it down."

King Anemi watched his hair be fashioned into an attractive yet modest style.

Queen Revari reviewed him again. "There. Now you look perfect."

"Thank you. I haven't been to Maieman in ages. I'd rather not go."

"You have to see him. At least to tell him in a while for the final time."

King Anemi looked at her through the mirror again. "It's a shame I couldn't tell my husband that."

Queen Revari leaned down over his shoulder, staring at him in the mirror. "Yes. I know the feeling."

Picking up on the irritation in her tone, King Anemi asked, "Why were you on Lucian's craft, Revari? When I scanned Dora's memories, I saw you get on it. You were in uniform."

"I was a soldier in Father's army, Vivant. It's no secret."

"Yes, but you had resigned by the time the uniforms changed. And the guards only wore that style during the years you were in the Chamber of Despair. None were assigned to you."

Revari silently cursed. "Did Dora say it was me?"

"No. As I said, I saw you when I scanned her memories."

"Then obviously you're mistaken, Vivant. Keep in mind you were under the influence of Callidut. The effect could take years to wear off. If I were you, I wouldn't trust anything your mind interprets."

What a sneaky little devil you are, granddaughter.

He'd let it go. For now. Once he got to Maieman, he'd have more than enough time to turn the Krons against her.

"You're right. I guess I'm bound to live with the ramifications for a while."

He turned to her. "Why did you come? Are the flowers for Queen Marietta?"

Queen Revari watched a group of blue jays eat from a bird feeder. "Hell no. They're for you. You know I'd never allow another WomanForm to have Mother's roses."

Giving him a side-eyed glance, she said, "You may love your mother-in-law, but you wouldn't give these to her either, knowing how special they were to Mother. Consider this a peace offering."

"An offering of peace? From you?" He chuckled. "You've been wanting me dead for years. What's changed, Revari?"

"Grandfather Carlomon showed me the good times we had when we lived with him. You used to sing me to sleep and play with me. When I took my first steps, I walked to you."

She turned to him. "I was happy there, and the Carogues loved me. We would've had a good life had we remained on Coldarius."

The blue jays caught her attention again. "But King Dubian destroyed it all. Had he left us alone, we'd all be a lot happier than we are now."

"But you never would've met..." He paused, determined not to make a mistake.

What was that odious creature's name?!

"Oliver," he said. "And you wouldn't have your son."

"And you wouldn't have married General Kron. Gallium might've been our father."

"Gallium?!" spat King Anemi. "He's a commoner! You mean Dimaro!"

Queen Revari looked at her as if she were crazy. "Dimaro?! As loathsome and repulsive as he was? Mother never would've married that animal! You really must be worried about King Micah to spew such nonsense!"

King Anemi trained his attention on rearranging the items on the vanity to hide his rage. "I find a princess marrying a commoner to be laughable. Prince Dimaro was her equal. They would've been married had Dubian not interfered!"

Queen Revari snorted. "Her equal? That's like comparing an eagle to a snake. Only in King Anemi's rabid mind was that a good match!"

She filled a small pot with water and poured it into the vase. "Gallium told me Coldarius wasn't as snooty as Platirius. It wasn't unusual for commoners to marry royalty. Our grandmother Elia was a NurseForm when she met Grandfather Carlomon."

Queen Revari looked at him quizzically. "Vivant, you saw how Dimaro was. Do you actually believe Mother would've been happy with that sociopath?"

King Anemi knew if he said anything more, she'd grow suspicious. "Well, they're dead now. I see no reason to bring up the past."

Queen Revari pointed at him. "Now you're sounding more like yourself. Always ready to bury your head in the sand when something painful comes up. But you can't hide from what's going on with King Micah."

"That's true," he said, rising. "I should get going. Thank you for the roses."

"No problem. I would say give my love to the Krons, but I have none to give them."

He hid a smile. *I'll just bet you don't.* "I understand, Revari."

"I'll let myself out," said Queen Revari. "In a while."

"In a while," muttered King Anemi. He took one of the roses from the expensive vase, twirling it around in his hand.

"How dare you insult my son?" Gripping the stem so tightly, he didn't notice the thorns cutting into his hand until a ribbon of blood seeped through his fingers.

"Damn!" he said when a few spots of blood dripped onto the dress.

"Queen Vivant, the craft is waiting!" called Advisor TamRi. "Are you ready?"

"Yes, I'm coming!" he called.

He forcefully pushed the rose back into the vase and grabbed a towel to staunch the blood. Tossing it on the bed, he straightened the day gown and observed his reflection in the mirror.

"The real question is, are the Krons ready for me?"

H e struggled not to show contempt for Maieman's luxurious splendor. He had expected it to be modest. It wasn't. The palace's walls shimmered with sparkling topaz. Its tall columns and high, abstract rooftops gave it a modernistic feel.

He noted the road to the main entrance was paved in platinum and topaz. The lush orchards filled with avocado, pear, lime, lemon, and mango trees looked peaceful and inviting.

The princesses were impressed by enchanted fish, covered in pure emerald and diamond scales, swimming in ice-blue ponds. Queen Marietta met them at the main gate.

"Vivant," she said tearfully, hugging King Anemi. "I'm so happy to see you. Thank you for coming so quickly."

King Anemi half-heartedly embraced her while looking around at the sprawling palace. It pained him to know King Micah had given his family an extraordinary life.

"Well," he said, standing back to peruse her. "You've done well for yourself."

Confusion marred her regal face. "Excuse me? What do you mean, Vivant? You've been here many times."

"I mean under the circumstances," he said smoothly. "I can imagine how much it must be killing you to see him this way."

Queen Marietta frowned. She'd never heard her daughter-in-law speak that way before. Perhaps it was all the pressure she'd been under ruling Platirius without a husband.

Spotting the blood on her skirt, she asked, "What happened? How did you hurt yourself?"

"Oh, I cut myself on a rose. I didn't have time to clean up."

Queen Marietta stared at him. She'd never known the younger queen to leave a stain on her clothes—no matter the reason. "Come. You must be exhausted from the trip. Let's get you and my granddaughters comfortable."

"Grandmother!" said Princess Teenah, running to embrace her.

"Teenah! By The One, you are so beautiful, my darling! Beauty times three," she said, opening her arms to receive hugs from the triplets. "You don't know how happy it makes me to see all of you here. I've wanted you all here with us for so long."

She looked at Queen Vivant. "I think Lucian would want you to live here too. I wish you had come the moment he disappeared."

Inwardly, King Anemi fumed. *Give up my grand palace? For this?*

"We've been through this before. Platirius is home, Mother."

The princesses looked at their mother strangely. She'd never taken that tone with Queen Marietta before.

The elder queen nodded. "Yes, well. Let's get you all inside, hm? I know seeing you will lift Micah's spirits."

Hopefully he'll lift up into the realm of The One right in front of me, thought King Anemi.

K ing Micah was lying quietly in his bed when the princesses entered with Queen Marietta.

"Micah? Look who's here?" said Queen Marietta. "Vivant! And she's brought our granddaughters to see you!"

He stretched his arms wide to receive the princesses. They gathered around him, planting kisses on his cheeks.

Princess Tarah grasped his arm. His skin was dry and slightly cool to the touch. "How are you feeling, Grandfather?"

He cleared his throat. "Now that I've seen you, my heart is soaring. All of you are so lovely! A perfect mesh of Lucian and Vivant."

He looked up just as King Anemi entered. "Vivant? How are you?"

King Anemi sat next to him, careful not to take his hand.

"I wish I could say I was better. But seeing you like this isn't something I expected. You've always been so strong and vital. Please get better for us, Father?"

"I've been trying, but I don't think The One wants to let me stay. No matter what happens, please know I love you and my granddaughters very much. I've made financial arrangements for all of you. Once they reach twenty-five summers, their assets will be released to them. They're separate from the funds I'm transitioning to you."

"Let's not talk about that now, Father. What's important is that we're all here together," said King Anemi.

"Marietta, can you show our granddaughters around? I'd like to speak with Vivant alone."

"Of course, my love. Come, let's go and see what the dining staff has prepared for dinner."

When the door closed, King Micah grabbed his elbow, staring at King Anemi for several seconds.

"What the hell are you doing in my daughter-in-law's body, Anemi?"

Chapter 3

King Anemi tried to snatch his arm away, but gripping him with a strength that surprised the dark king, King Micah sat up straight in his bed.

"You've always thought your skill in black magic was superior to everyone. I gave it up to marry Marietta, but don't you think for one second you're fooling me! Why are you not in Hell where you belong?"

King Anemi smirked. "If you tell a soul what you know, your granddaughters will be vacationing there long before me."

"Who will stop me? We both know you can't kill me. If you do, Maieman will be absorbed into Platirius. What are you up to?"

"You'll be dead before you find out, so why worry?"

He looked down at the offending hand. "Let go before I break your fingers!"

"I want you the hell away from my family!"

"My family, Micah. Mine! I have plans for Vivant and her daughters."

King Micah pointed a finger at his face. "If you hurt them," he warned.

"I'm back to take what's mine. Platirius. No one has to get hurt." He snatched his arm away from the dying king. "Not that it's any of your concern. My business is resurrection and yours? Dying. Just like your son."

"How dare you?!" roared King Micah.

He wished he had the strength to punch a grinning King Anemi.

"Queen Revari killed him, you know? She got on his craft and drugged him, then sent him flying right into the sun. That's why you've never found a body."

Black eyes met gray. "And you never will. Your son is gone. Forever."

"You're trash, Anemi!"

It unnerved King Micah to see his wicked smile on Queen Vivant's face.

"I may be mendacious, but it's true. I can help you get revenge against Revari."

King Micah lay back down on the bed. "We don't need your help to avenge my son. You want me to help you get rid of Revari so you'll have a straight shot to Platirius. I may be dying, but I'm not blind, Anemi. I'll never help you take Platirius back. As cursed as it is, it belongs to Vivant!"

"The thought of a WomanForm ruling my kingdom sickens me."

"Not more than your presence has sickened me over the years. I'll never help you."

King Anemi shrugged. "Then you'll die knowing I'm still alive and well. I really don't need you to spearhead an attack against Revani. Jonah and Marietta will be more than willing to do it."

King Micah's eyes closed to slits. "You won't use my family for your sick games."

"What are you going to do about it? If you tell anyone how you know what you know, you'll have to reveal your past to Marietta." He leaned in close to King Micah's face. "And I'm sure that's a secret you're willing to take with you to the grave, old friend."

He stood, staring down at a furious King Micah. "It seems this is what we call a conundrum. The best part is I get to watch you draw your last breath and spend the inheritance funds you've gifted to Vivant and her brats. I'd say the ball is in my court."

King Micah looked at him solemnly. "For now. My body is dying, but I still know a few tricks. Even now, I can make life miserable for you, Anemi."

King Anemi smiled. "I'm shaking. I'm also hungry. I can't wait to see what's for supper."

Queen Marietta noticed Queen Vivant had barely said two words after they sat down to eat.

"Vivant, I had the chefs prepare all of your favorites!"

King Anemi looked at the large variety of dishes and frowned. "Where's the curried carrot bisque?"

"Curried carrot bisque?" asked Queen Marietta. "Since when do you eat carrots?"

The Krons and the princesses stared at King Anemi, waiting for an answer.

"Uh. King Asa's chef served it once. After I tasted it, I found I liked it."

Noting Queen Marietta silently studying him, he said, "It doesn't matter. We have quite the spread here. Thank you, Mother."

Prince Jonah cleared his throat. "Well, I hope you'll like the food, princesses. We had to mash up everything for you the last time you were here. I can't believe you're twenty summers now."

Princess Teenah rubbed her hands together. "We intend to do all of this justice. Right, sisters?"

Her sisters agreed. Unlike their mother, the princesses were quite pleased to see appetizers of fried calamari, portobello mushroom caps stuffed with herbed breadcrumbs and crab, along with a fresh salad with grape tomatoes, olives, feta, and shrimp. Princess Tarah passed the small pot of tangy lemon and thyme dressing to her grandmother.

The main course was exactly what you'd expect to see on a royal table: stuffed lobster tails, medium well steaks, broccoli roasted with parmesan, shrimp paella, lobster and avocado salad, and pasta shells stuffed with spinach and ricotta in a creamy white wine and shallot sauce.

Princess Tyre had a penchant for sweets. She was pleased to see her favorite chocolate cake covered in chocolate Swiss meringue buttercream. A strawberry Chantilly cake frosted in mounds of whipped cream stood waiting to be sliced into.

They ate in silence for a few moments before King Anemi asked, "What happened to the large timekeeper that used to sit in the corner?"

Queen Marietta gaped at her. "That timekeeper was moved before Lucian reached his thirteenth summer. Vivant, how could you possibly know that?"

Silently, King Anemi swore.

Captain Josin's surly mood hadn't lifted since he woke up. Surrounded by the veteran JanIan soldiers, he angrily spat on the ground.

"That was his plan all along—to take out our king! The thought of being ruled by a Human makes me sick!"

"He's half Human," said Sergeant Amara. "I don't understand why you have a gripe against him. He saved us from being taken over by King Belial."

He whirled on her. "Better to be ruled by him than a Human—half or not! Now he's brought in these Coldarian soldiers! Who do you think he'll show favor to, huh?"

"Were it not for Coldarius, we wouldn't be here," Sergeant Amara countered. "I don't see this as an us versus them when we're all the same."

He advanced toward her. "We're *not* the same," he said through clenched teeth. "We are JanIans! The One fashioned our first two ancestors with his own hands and set them here after Coldarius exploded. The CarogueStone gave JanIus life, but it was He who breathed it into them! Most of the Coldarians were long dead when that happened."

"Captain, you're splitting hairs. Just admit you hate King Justin and be done with it."

"Alright. I hate him. There. I said it. Are you satisfied?"

She shook her head. "No, I'm not. Actually, I'm disappointed. If we don't work as a team, our enemies will have no problem defeating us."

"Have you forgotten that I'm the captain of this army, Sergeant? I don't need *you* to tell *me* how to run it!"

He turned to face the other soldiers. "Have you thought about our enemies? They've increased now that everyone knows we're ruled by Human blood! It's only a matter of time before someone takes over JanIus again!"

"Only if our army has weak leadership," she muttered under her breath.

"What did you just say?" asked Captain Josin. "Stand at attention, soldier!"

He got in her face. "I asked, what did you just say?"

The atmosphere in the military chamber grew menacing when their eyes locked. If she voiced her opinion out loud, she'd get hit with a demerit for insubordination. And, she knew the captain, a staunch misogynist, would make her life hell.

"Nothing."

"What's that? I didn't hear you."

"I said nothing!"

"Say it again. Louder and not under your breath like a spineless coward!"

"Nothing!" she shouted.

"That's right. You said nothing because you *are* nothing! We've never had WomenForms in this army before King Leighton appointed you and we don't need you now."

He smiled at her. "In fact, now that he's gone, I see no reason for you to stay. All the Coldarian soldiers are MaleForms, and I've heard the king wants to recruit Gallium to be his general. Except for you and that doctor, I don't think he'll add any more of your kind. It'll be easy to get you out."

He blew a lock of hair out of her face. She wrinkled her nose when his bad breath hit her nostrils.

"I'm still the highest rank. Even if the Coldarian leads us, I have no doubt I'll be appointed colonel. I can still make your life as miserable as I please."

He flicked her forehead with his finger. "So if I were you, I'd shut my mouth and get with the program. No matter who sits on that throne, WomenForms will never be equal to us!"

51

She scanned the hostile faces of her male comrades. They were in complete agreement with the captain. She realized they'd left her alone while King Leighton was alive, but things could change very quickly.

"Sergeant Amara. It's time to clean the bath chambers. Lucky for you, one of the soldiers got stone-cold drunk and vomited everywhere. Be careful where you step."

It wasn't her turn to clean them. She knew he had singled her out on purpose. Giving a crisp salute, she pivoted swiftly toward the bath chambers. Venomous laughter followed her. No one noticed Sergeant Lionus quickly exiting the military chamber.

"Ki̇ng Justin wants you to do what?" asked General Legend.

"You heard me the first time, Legend. He's asked me to be his general."

They were sitting in Queen Revari's elegant library. She set aside the book she'd been reading. "Are you considering it?"

"Yes," said Gallium. "I think I would be more helpful on JanIus than here. You have Legend leading your army. My job is making weapons, and I can do that while I'm on Revani. King Justin knows I don't want to live apart from Legend. He assured me I can travel between the planets freely."

Queen Revari surveyed him carefully. "It sounds as if you've already made up your mind. I hope I didn't offend you when I said you'd never hold a leadership position in my army."

"No, My Queen. I wasn't offended—then or now. I understand why you said it."

"Then is it for executing Dr. Barrios? Things couldn't remain as they were. Surely you understand he'd broken our most sacred laws. And he had it coming for murdering my aunt."

"I've never held that against you," said Gallium. "Wait. He did what?"

"Dr. Barrios slit her throat and tried to blame Vivant for it. King Dubian took the blade from her and put it in the soldier's hand—the one he pinned her murder on. I saw it all. I think had Dr. Barrios seen me, he would've killed me too."

Gallium slowly lowered himself beside General Legend. She leaned forward, stroking his back.

"I've never known you to be at a loss for words," she said. "Tell us what's on your mind."

"But why? Why would he kill Queen Opal?"

Queen Revari's heart ached for him. "He blamed her and my mother for the deaths of your parents. And for losing Coldarius."

He turned to his wife. "Did you know he killed Queen Opal?"

She moved a lock of hair off his cheek. "Not until this moment."

Gallium sighed deeply. "You did what had to be done, Your Highness. No one is above the law."

Why didn't I see how far you were gone, Ezra?

General Legend hugged him. "It wasn't your fault. Dr. Barrios made his own choices. It wasn't your responsibility to save him."

Gallium shook his head to clear it. He didn't want to talk about his brother.

"The truth is, I miss fighting in battles sometimes. When I'm not making weapons, I sit around like a potted plant until I'm needed."

General Legend held his hand firmly in hers. Seeing him express conflicting emotions was a rare experience. She hated when she couldn't help him.

"Life hasn't changed for me since we were on Rubarius," he said. "I'm not saying I'm ungrateful. I just miss the way my old life used to be. I miss socializing with MaleForms."

Queen Revari crossed her ankles. "There's more. No one knows you better than Legend and I. Please share it with us."

"Alright. When I was stuck in that hole, dying, I heard Queen Dellah's voice. She told me it was all right to let go."

"What does that mean?" asked Queen Revari.

"When you were born, I promised her I'd never leave your side. Not until your death. I meant every word. I've tried to keep my promise, but I know I've failed her...and you...and Queen Vivant."

He squeezed General Legend's hand. "I've never considered you a burden—you mean more to me than you could imagine. But when she told me I could let go, I felt free. Seeing King

Carlomon again, knowing Coldarius isn't under Platirius's shadow anymore gave me peace too."

He knelt in front of the queen. "You don't need me here, but JanIus does. Justin is far too green. He doesn't know how to be a king, and if it's to survive—and I'm sure that's what we all want—he'll need my help."

"I agree," said Queen Revari and General Legend.

He stared at her, then at his wife. "What?"

She shrugged. "We just agreed. Before you walked in here, Legend and I were wondering if you'd help him. Had I known you made a pact with my mother, I would've eased your conscience a long time ago. I appreciate you looking after me for all these years, but I don't need a MaleForm to protect me. My army can go up against any king in Space. I can't see anyone leading it other than my sister, Legend."

Moved by the compliment, General Legend averted her head to hide her tears.

"I must admit, I don't like what happened between you and Colonel Angela. The last thing I need is infighting among my troops. So, I release you from working under me. You may go to JanIus and return here to spend time with your lovely wife. Justin doesn't realize he'll have endless enemies—both living and dead—coming for him for the rest of his lifespan. I'd feel better knowing you were at his side."

The TeleShield buzzed.

"My Queen, I've brought refreshments."

"Come in."

A dining staff brought in a large pitcher of sangria and lemon rolls. After bowing to the queen, she made a quick exit.

Queen Revari waited for Gallium to pour their drinks. "Only the three of us know Vivant and I saved JanIus from financial ruin after King Leighton's gambling debts spiraled out of control. I intend to use it to further my mother's vision. So, there's something else I want before you go, Gallium."

"Name it, My Queen."

Licking icing from her fingertips, she smiled at General Legend.

He shook his head. "What have the two of you been up to while I was gone?"

After hearing the sisters' uproarious laughter, he braced himself for the news.

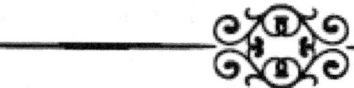

T he pinning on ceremony had nearly finished. King Justin sat on his throne, watching the soldiers step forward to receive their promotions.

"There are just a few more special advancements I'd like to announce," he said.

Captain Josin, Sergeant Lionus, Sergeant Amara, and Sergeant Azini, step forth, please?"

The four approached the throne and kneeled before him.

"Three of you fought bravely against King Belial, and some have shown unyielding loyalty to me. I think it's important for everyone here to see you receive the fruit of your labor."

He turned to Gallium and General Legend. "My two honored guests have been gracious enough to assist me in rebuilding my army. Please welcome your new general, Gallium Barrios. I'm honored he decided to accept my offer."

The spectators focused on the tall, well-built MaleForm standing next to the king.

"When King Leighton was alive, I was inspired by how he handled things. His progressive vision should never be forgotten. Therefore, my army will be formed with an equal number of the SexForms."

Someone gasped in the audience, while Captain Josin flinched.

"You may stand, Captain Josin," the king commanded.

He waited for the captain to look him in the eye before he said, "It's come to my attention you've been mistreating some of the soldiers. Not only does it concern me, it angers me to my core. You have much to learn about how to treat Beings, so I'm demoting you to private."

"What?"

Gallium stepped forward, unsheathing his sword. "You dare speak out of turn to your king?"

Captain Josin paled, falling silent. King Justin looked at General Legend.

"General Legend is the commander of the Revaltian army. She's agreed to stay with us for a short while and train new female recruits who'd like to join mine. I'm promoting Sergeant Amara to captain and Sergeant Azini to colonel. Soldiers, please stand and be recognized."

Loud applause flooded the hall for the first two females to hold high ranks in the JanIan army. Still hungover from the previous night's round of binge drinking, Musha Azini watched from a distance, her arms hanging limply at her side.

The new colonel and captain bowed to King Justin, honored by the appointments.

Fawn's radiant face made his heart beat faster. "My great-grandfather believed in the progression of WomenForms. So do I. I've witnessed more atrocities committed against them than I'd like to admit. Please understand, I intend to root out every hint of misogyny in my kingdom. There's no place for it here."

Observing the large crowd, he said, "The old way is gone. Either fall in line with my vision, or leave. I won't warn you again. General Legend, would you like to say anything?"

"Yes, thank you, King Justin." Gracing the audience with her beautiful smile, she said, "Well, I'm very excited to be here. You may not know this, but I'm one of the original Coldarians. Seeing an extension of it thriving warms my heart more than you know."

She held up two fingers. "In two summers, I'll recruit and train WomenForms for King Justin's army. This was a dream of his grandmother, Queen Dellah of Platirius. Her daughter, Queen Revari, has graciously appointed me to bring her mother's vision to life."

A large cluster of WomenForms grasping each other's hands made her smile. Their excitement made her remember how it felt when she learned she'd become a soldier too.

"Queen Dellah trained me when I joined Coldarius's army. I can't tell you what an honor it is to share this moment with you, her descendants."

She clapped her hands together. "So! Recruitment applications have been downloaded onto your personal hard drives. If any female is interested in joining the king's army, please complete the application and submit all of the required documentation. If you're selected, you'll be notified by the end of next week. Thank you."

Another round of applause followed the general's speech. Next, it was Gallium's turn.

"I think King Justin and General Legend have pretty much covered everything. I just want to say I'm happy to join JanIus's army, and I look forward to helping the king rebuild it. I agree with him—misogyny isn't welcome among us. If I see it, you're gone. As for the WomenForms, please understand you'll be treated no differently than the MaleForms. I expect you to work hard and get along with your fellow troops. Thank you."

Not one for saying much, he stepped back into place beside King Justin.

"There's one more appointment. I'm also promoting Sergeant Lionus to colonel too. JanIus's record in battle is undefeated. Next to General Barrios, his experience is vital to ensuring we keep it that way."

He nodded to Colonel Lionus after his medals were pinned on him. "Welcome aboard, Colonel."

The colonel saluted him. "Thank you, King Justin!"

The king trained his attention on Private Josin. "What's the matter, Private? You look ill."

Private Josin struggled to find his voice. "N–no, Your Highness. I feel fine."

King Justin's malevolent stare pinned him in place. "I've appointed a male and a female colonel, but that doesn't mean you'll obey Colonel Leighton and ignore Colonel Azini. Are we clear on that?"

His glacial tone struck fear in Private Josin's heart. Captain Amara wanted to laugh, yet held her composure. It was more than enough to know he'd answer to *her* now.

"Yes, My King!"

"Good dog, Josin!"

Gallium's and General Legend's eyes shifted to the king.

"Who does he sound like?" General Legend whispered to Gallium. "Queen Dellah," they said in unison.

Scanning the rows of soldiers, King Justin said, "Let this be your first and final warning. Disobey my orders, and you may not be lucky enough to get a demotion. I may be inclined to end you in front of everyone you love. That's all for now. Please report to your stations. And remember, on JanIus, we're one united family. May The One bless us all."

On Revani, Queen Revari watched the ceremony with Colonels Angela and Sheila. They lifted their glasses in a toast.

"I'll drink to that, my friends!" she said.

A visitor sat quietly, their eyes cast downward.

The queen's supercilious smile hit its mark. "It's time for you to earn your keep. Not even The One will find your bones if you cross me."

"Yes, My Queen."

King Micah's breath was slow and unsteady. Sickened by King Anemi's perverted abuse of spiritual power, his mind raced to think of a way to free Queen Vivant. Following the chime of the TeleShield, Queen Marietta entered.

"I've come to sit with you, so don't tell me to leave. I want to spend every moment I can with you."

He reached for her. "I wouldn't dream of it. Come and sit with me, my love."

She sat and bathed his face with a lavender-scented cloth. "I want you to fight to stay with me, Micah. We have too many years left before you visit The One."

He removed the cloth from her hand and kissed it. "No, we don't, Marietta. I'm dying. I've accepted it. You must too."

"But..."

"No buts," he said, softly but firmly. "Jonah will take my place as we planned. Now listen to me...there's something I must tell you. I'll understand if you leave me to die alone."

Gently gripping the sides of his face, she asked, "What on Maieman are you talking about, old king?"

"We don't have much time. Vivant and our granddaughters are in trouble. And...I now know what happened to our son."

She grasped his shoulders. "Lucian? What happened? Where is he?"

"Queen Revari drugged him and sent his craft into the sun."

He grabbed her hands when she tried to pull away. "That's why we've never found a body, Marietta."

"But why? Why would she kill him?" she cried.

"She blamed him for murdering her husband."

"The Human? But that was King Dubian's doing. Lucian was just following orders! That little witch! She must be brought before our council!"

"That can never happen," said King Micah.

"Why not, Micah?!"

"Because...she's the only one who can save Vivant now. Her...and her halfling son."

K ing Anemi roamed the halls of the palace, snubbing his nose at most of the furnishings and décor.

"By The One, Micah, did you have to let Marietta turn your halls into a female haven? One would never know MaleForms lived here."

He paused to scowl at a particularly beautiful painting of the king and queen before setting his sights on a family portrait. General Kron and Prince Jonah stood behind their seated parents. The third painting captured Queen Vivant standing with the Krons. Her three small princesses stood at her knees, tugging on her gown. The happy family smiled into the camera.

"Mother!" cried Princess Tyre. "Tarah got out of the shower without washing her feet!"

Without taking his eyes off the painting, King Anemi said, "What does that have to do with me?"

Dumbfounded, she stared at him. She had expected her sister to be scolded. Nothing irritated their mother more than uncleanliness.

"She's dressed now and says she doesn't have to wash them. Please make her!"

Princess Tarah rushed into the study. "Mother, I washed well. I don't like when Tyre polices what I do!" Turning to her sister, she said, "You don't set the standard on cleanliness!"

Princess Tyre narrowed her eyes. "You're right. Mother does! And she's always told us we need to scrub every part of our bodies! That includes behind our ears and in between our toes! It's disgraceful for you to be this gross!"

Princess Tarah's temper flared. "Let me tell you something, you—"

He slightly shifted his body toward them. "You're twenty summers, yet you're quarreling over how to bathe properly? Are you more useless than kakapos?"

Shocked, the princesses stared at their mother. She'd never spoken to them that way.

King Anemi eyed Princess Tarah as if he were sizing her up to be beheaded.

"Return to the bath chamber and don't return until you've washed every inch of your body. I have enough on my mind without you running around here shaming me with this nonsense! Get out of my sight. Both of you!"

Princess Tarah's lip trembled while tears smarted in her sister's eyes.

"Go!" roared King Anemi.

They hurried away from him, succumbing to tears.

Princess Tarah angrily wiped hers away. "Do you see what you've done? Mother is under a lot of strain and you made her scold us like ChildForms!"

Princess Tyre shook her head in wonder. "She's never been cross with us before."

Princess Tarah sniffed. "Grandfather is ill. That's what's bothering her. She doesn't want to lose him like she lost Father."

"I won't bring anything else to her attention if you promise to bathe like she taught us!"

Princess Tarah disrobed and snatched a bathing cloth from the walk-in closet. "I will now. I hope you're satisfied, Tyre!"

Princess Tarah stormed into the bath chamber, leaving Princess Tyre sitting on the bed, reflecting on her mother's strange mood. "I thought things would be better if we came to see Grandfather. But I'm not satisfied with the way things are going. Not at all."

General Lyric had just returned from a run when she spied a WomanForm sitting on the ground. Wiping sweat from her face and neck, she passed her and entered her small cottage.

By the time she had showered and changed clothes, she was still there. After hastily throwing together roast chicken sandwiches, she turned the heat off under a pot of corn chowder and sighed.

"What is she still doing out there? And who is she?"

She removed dishes from the cupboard and set them on the table, yet she wouldn't be able to eat with her sitting outside. She liked having her personal space. She'd purchased the 450 acres from the queen years ago. There was no reason for anyone to intrude on her little slice of heaven.

"Just get it over with, Lyric," she muttered. Snatching open the door, she cautiously approached the WomanForm. "Excuse me, are you lost? This is private property—you can't sit out here alone."

The WomanForm removed the satin hood from her head.

No! It can't be!

She hadn't seen her in years. All the memories she'd thought were forgotten came flooding back.

"Hello, Lyric. It's Mama," said Lady Alarah.

King Asa was in a foul mood. He had no quarrel with King Micah, but it irritated him that he chose to die during the time he would've spent with Queen Vivant. He couldn't forget how strange she sounded when he'd spoken with her.

What if another MaleForm has captured her interest? No. That's not it. Vivant would tell me if that were the case. Then why do I feel something is wrong?

He started to call her, then changed his mind. She was probably under a lot of pressure—he didn't want to add to her burden by acting like a jealous lover. Yet, that's exactly how he felt.

Prince Jonah would be crowned king after his father passed. She'd been married to his brother, but was it possible they'd struck up a connection? Or she'd marry him out of duty? He didn't like where his mind was going.

"No," he said. "If she wanted to abandon Platirius for Maieman, she would've done it years ago. Get ahold of yourself, Asa. You haven't been this anxious since your TeenForm years."

He found it difficult to focus. To his surprise, he'd fallen in love with her. How else could he explain feeling sick to his stomach when he was in perfect health? He groaned. All he could do was wait for her to call him.

Stepping into the warm sun, he made his way toward his grand stables. "I'm going for a ride. Hold all calls, except those from Maieman. If it's the queen, come and find me immediately."

"Yes, My King," said a soldier. "We were expecting her today. Will she visit again soon?"

To King Asa, the sun looked as if it were turning blood red. "She has no reason not to," he said. But as he climbed on his favorite stallion, a tiny shred of doubt crept into his mind. "She'll be back."

Won't she?

Chapter 4

Queen Marietta awoke in her husband's arms. She'd lost count of the number of times they'd fallen asleep together. She looked up into peaceful visage.

"Wherever you are, My King, wait for me. I'll join you soon."

The death bells for King Micah sounded throughout the halls. Soldiers and groups of staff in the work chambers streamed out, headed for the front of the palace to mourn their fallen king. Queen Marietta found Prince Jonah in his bed chamber, looking out at the mourners. He didn't turn around when she entered.

"I don't want to see the pain in your eyes, nor do I want you to see it in mine. I keep telling myself if I stand here long enough, I'll see him sitting in the garden, feeding his birds."

The queen placed a hand on his shoulder.

"I never wanted to be king, Mother. I always thought Lucian would return home so I wouldn't have to. Now I know he won't, and I finally know why."

He turned to her. "From what you say, there's nothing we can do to bring her to justice. Do you know how hard it is for me not to go to Revani and drag her here?"

"Believe me, son, I know. But if we retaliate against her, we'll lose Vivant and her daughters. As a mother, I have to love Vivant more than I hate Revari. Lucian is gone—we can't bring him back. I refuse to lose her too."

"What hope do we have of getting her back?"

"Micah said Anemi has interfered with The One's laws. Vivant and Revari's advisors are soldiers in His army. His dark power has no effect on them. If we work together, we may defeat him and free Vivant from his spell."

"I've had Father moved to the worship chamber. Following his DeathCeremony, I'll be coronated as king. Under normal circumstances, we'd wait for the usual mourning period to pass, but all of us are in danger. We need to move fast." His jaw tightened. "It's been hard as hell to pretend I don't know it's not Vivant."

"We must. We have to protect my granddaughters. They're all we have left of Lucian. If he suspects we know what he's up to, there's no telling what he'll do."

"You're right, Mother. It's killing me not to share this with them."

"It's for their own safety. They love Vivant, and they've just lost Micah. I suspect Tarah hasn't made amends with losing Lucian—it's too much to ask them to keep it a secret."

Prince Jonah kissed her on the cheek. "I'll meet you in the worship chamber shortly."

After she left, he took off his clothes and stepped into the shower. Angrily scrubbing his skin with a bathing cloth, he recalled all the times he and his brother had played together in the palace's halls.

"When all of this is over, I'm coming to get you, Queen Revari. You *will* pay for what you did to my brother!"

The soft lighting of the worship chamber created a calming effect. The princesses were seated next to King Anemi—all were dressed in royal-blue day gowns. The fashionable netted hats perched on top of their heads were the perfect complement. Per Queen Marietta's request, Tese Blight had shipped the clothes overnight.

Contrary to her daughter-in-law and granddaughters, the Queen of Maieman wore a powder-blue day gown with a matching tignon. Dressed in all black, Prince Jonah's regal entrance made everyone take notice. Pausing at his father's DeathCraft, he bowed his head to pay his respects.

"Thank you for all you've done, Father. Don't worry. You know I'll protect them with my life."

He sat next to Queen Marietta as the service began. Candid videos of King Micah's life flashed across the large TranScreen. Everyone laughed when a young Micah, just three summers, got into hair cream and smeared it over his face. As the images transitioned, showing various stages of his life, King Anemi's face was as still as stone.

It was a credit to his cunning ways that he'd chosen Queen Vivant for a host. By nature, she was prone to showing very little emotion. Past trauma had taught her to suppress her feelings. It was the perfect cover. Everyone paused when the screen suddenly went black. Prince Jonah shot a glance at one of the surveillance staff.

"What's going on?" he mouthed.

Before the staff could react, another video appeared. Queen Marietta gasped.

The video of General Kron admitting the part he played in destroying Coldarius shot across the screen. Queen Marietta stood, her mouth hanging open. The next scene was of him sitting in a craft, speeding toward the sun. Breathing harshly and sweating profusely, he desperately tried to reach something with his finger. The princesses bolted forward, their eyes fixed on their father.

"Ah!" he cried after finding a small button on his safety belt. Princess Teenah covered her mouth with one hand while squeezing Princess Tarah's hand with the other.

The seat bolted upward, ejecting him from the craft just before it was engulfed in a fiery inferno. A small portable surveillance screen captured the general hurling fast toward a rocky area surrounded by water. His parachute opened, but not in time to prevent him from diving into the raging waves. Then the screen went black.

Anxious shouts and furious whispers filled the worship chamber as everyone tried to make sense of what they'd just seen.

What? General Kron helped King Dubian kill the Coldarians?!

He betrayed Queen Vivant's family, and she still married him? How could she?

By The One! Does this mean he's still alive?

I don't doubt it. He probably couldn't face what he did and chose to hide all of this time!

But that's ridiculous! He wouldn't abandon his ChildForms!

I wouldn't have thought he'd help to murder Coldarians, but here we are!

Prince Jonah stood. "Please be quiet, everyone!" he said. "That's enough!" he shouted when the noise grew more intense.

"How dare you sully the name of a royal?"

The crowd wilted under his furious gaze. "This footage wasn't a part of my father's DeathCeremony! We don't know if it's legit, and here you sit, ready to tear my brother apart! I won't have you gossiping about him when our father's body is lying not even a foot away!"

King Anemi kept his eyes on the floor, thoroughly enjoying witnessing Queen Marietta's world crash and burn at her feet.

Prince Jonah pointed to the surveillance staff. "I want to know where that footage came from and how it got onto that screen! Now!" he roared.

Queen Marietta surveyed her husband's vessel through blurred vision.

The disrespect!

Rousing himself, King Anemi rushed to play his role.

"Mother? Please, allow me?"

Queen Marietta nearly stiffened at his touch, but collected herself.

King Anemi stood in front of the worship chamber.

"This is the highest form of disrespect to a royal. A DeathCeremony is supposed to be a celebration of life and honor. Yet, clearly, someone holds a grudge against my father-in-law. My husband's guilt or innocence shouldn't be the focus here. Many of you do the lowest grunt work and it's fitting that you should! You aren't royalty, you're commoners. Destined to eat the scraps that drop from our table. We will not tolerate you forgetting your place!"

The princesses stared at their mother. Prince Jonah took a step forward.

"Vivant! I'll handle this!" he said through clenched teeth.

King Anemi's impertinent gaze was plain. "You appeared to be struggling, Jonah. If you can't get your subjects in line, I don't mind showing you how it's done!"

Queen Marietta gripped the top of the seat. "Vivant, please sit down. You're only making things worse!"

King Anemi's mocking gaze swept over her.

He knows exactly what he's doing! He's trying to cause an uprising so our subjects will doubt Jonah's ability to lead Maieman. You disrespectful cur!

With an arrogant toss of his head, King Anemi took his place beside Queen Vivant's daughters. Shock and anger rippled through the DeathCeremony. He'd planted just enough animosity to sprout and take root.

Out of the corner of his eye, he spied the princesses. One had burst into tears, and another refused to look at him. But the one they called Tarah stared directly at him. Her eyes traveled from his feet to the top of his head, then into his eyes.

She knows something is wrong. The little whore!

He leaned in close to her. "Fix your face or I'll fix it for you, Teenah."

"I'm Tarah," she said briskly. "And my mother would never make that mistake!"

Queen Marietta shot a panicked look at Prince Jonah.

"Tarah, your mother has been under a lot of stress," he said quickly. "She's not herself. Let's get through father's service as a family, please?"

The rest of the DeathCeremony was as silent as a grave. After the death feast had been consumed and King Micah was finally laid to rest, Prince Jonah was quickly crowned the new King of Maieman.

Standing before his subjects, he said, "There's evil at work here, but it wasn't bred among my family. We have always led our Beings with pride and excellence. I ask that you hold fast to all of the good memories and the joy and prosperity we've brought you. Do not allow the events that unfolded today to sway your unwavering loyalty and support for us."

King Anemi scowled, watching the handsome king's charismatic spirit re-win the hearts and minds of his subjects.

"I don't know if my brother is dead or alive, but I promise I'll get to the bottom of it. And if he's alive, I'll bring him home to us. This is where he belongs."

Looking deeply into King Anemi's eyes, he said, "He never should've gone to Platirius, but what's done is done. My nieces deserve justice. I fully intend to see that they'll have it."

Observing the faces of his subjects—some hopeful, others crestfallen—motivated him to be a king they could be proud of.

"Thank you all for paying respect to my father's legacy. A new reign has come for Maieman. After today, my family's name will never be shamed again."

Ah, the brave and the foolish, thought King Anemi. *How insufferable.*

He swiped a carrot stick as the dining staff removed a vegetable tray from the table. Its crisp snap coincided with the sharpness of Queen Marietta and Princess Tarah's gazes.

"Mother?" asked General Lyric. "This can't be happening. It's not possible for you to be here right now."

"I've been gone for a long time, haven't I? I don't expect you to welcome me with open arms, but I just couldn't stay away from you forever. All I ask is for you to hear me out. If you want me to leave again, I will."

General Lyric could barely breathe. For years, she'd wanted to know what happened to her mother. Now she was standing in front of her. She couldn't form a coherent thought.

"Please come inside. I fixed a quick supper."

Lady Alarah smiled. "That sounds wonderful. Thank you, Lyric."

General Lyric led her into the cottage and removed another bowl and a saucer from the cupboard.

"Corn chowder and chicken sandwiches. Does that sound good?"

Lady Alarah sat down and removed her shawl. "After where I've been, it sounds like a feast. I'm grateful to you for taking me in."

She arranged the sandwiches and ladled soup into bowls. "All I have to drink is plum juice."

Lady Alarah nodded. "That's fine. Beggars shouldn't be choosy."

General Lyric sat down next to her. For a few moments, they ate in silence. The general couldn't take her eyes off her. Her face was still as beautiful as she remembered, except for a thin, jagged scar across her cheek.

"You know, your father used to stare at me that way," said Lady Alarah. "How is he?"

"He's dead. His craft blew up over Coldarius just before it exploded."

Lady Alarah nearly dropped her spoon. "Coldarius is gone?"

"Yes. It was absorbed into Platirius when I was a ChildForm. It was recently reabsorbed into JanIus."

"Reabsorbed? I've never heard of such a thing. I thought once a planet was taken, that was the end of it. And what is JanIus?"

The general added shredded cheese to her soup. "So did I, but that's not true. By some miracle, a piece of it broke off and formed another planet. JanIus is an extension of Coldarius."

Lady Alarah took a bite of the sandwich and smiled. "You put chives in the sandwich dressing. I've always loved it on my sandwiches."

"Father used to do it that way."

"I remember," said Lady Alarah quietly. "You say his craft blew up over the water. He didn't suffer, did he?"

"I don't know. I only recently learned what happened to him. My adoptive family told me you and he had died during a riding accident."

Lady Alarah stared at her. "Well, that was a lie. I apologize if it caused you pain."

General Lyric chewed thoughtfully. "And what about Domi? What about the pain you caused her?"

Lady Alarah's head snapped up. "Who?"

General Lyric took a sip of plum juice. "Your second daughter. You know? The baby you told everyone you lost?"

She fiddled with a napkin. "I was afraid to tell Iham when I found out I was carrying again. He wanted a second ChildForm so badly—I didn't want to break his heart."

"Mother, if you're going to sit there and lie to my face, I have no issue packing up your food and kicking you out of here! I'm not a ChildForm anymore, and I don't take well to lying."

Lady Alarah bit her bottom lip. "I know I have failed in my duties as a mother, Lyric, but I'd appreciate not being called a liar! I lost my son. I should know. I was there!"

"And where was I when you got pregnant by King Belial? You remember him, don't you?"

"Yes, I remember my sins well." Looking pointedly at General Lyric, she said, "I also remember who I slept with! This...Domi was my third InfantForm. Her father wasn't Belial, it was King Noham!"

"Then why did King Belial think she was his?"

Lady Alarah waved her hand. "Oh, he didn't. He was just too strange and too protective of his family to allow anyone to know I had seduced his father! Belial was a TeenForm when his father and I were together. Even I wouldn't lower myself to lie with an underage Being."

"That explains why he shot her in the back with no remorse."

Lady Alarah looked up from her bowl. "Then she's dead too?"

General Lyric grabbed another sandwich. "No, she lives on Onzi. King Asa's realm."

"Little Prince Asa became a king? I thought he was a third son. That's extremely rare."

"Queen Aiki killed off his brothers. His father eventually gave him the throne."

"I'm sure that killed King Alazar. Prince Asa wasn't his favorite son."

"What happened to Domi after she was born, Mother?"

"I couldn't explain her to Iham. We'd stopped copulating, so he would've known she wasn't his. But I couldn't bring myself to sweep her away. So I gave her to an orphanage and never looked back." She helped herself to another bowl of chowder. "I don't regret what I did. There was no place for her in my life."

"And what about me? You were alive during the time I was adopted. What did I do to become excess baggage?"

Lady Alarah looked at her sadly. "Oh, Lyric. You were never baggage to me."

General Lyric dropped her spoon into the empty bowl. "Then why did you give me up?"

"Things were complicated then, darling. I was trying to make life better—for both of us!"

"How?"

"Well, I figured if I married King Dubian, you would live in a palace and grow up with his daughters."

"But that isn't what happened. I was told the arrangement was you let go of me to get everything you wanted."

Lady Alarah's eyes hardened. "And who told you that? If everyone is gone, why would someone tell such a vicious lie?"

"It's not a lie. I never said all the Coldarians were gone. I said Coldarius was. There are more than a few Coldarians still alive and well! Do you remember Gallium Barrios and Legend Guilde?"

Lady Alarah swallowed. "How did they survive and not my Iham? Never mind! It doesn't matter. No one can know I'm here. If they discover I'm alive, they'll kill me!"

General Lyric cocked her head. "Are you serious? Mother, no one wants to kill you! You're being paranoid!"

"You don't know Gallium like I do! He's crazy! He hates me—he always has! Tell me, has he ever treated you with kindness? Even once?"

General Lyric remained silent.

"See? Gallium Barrios is just as wicked as King Dubian was! Lyric, I know I don't deserve an ounce of your love or support, but I'm telling the truth! Please hide me?"

She kneeled in front of her. "I've just reconnected with you! I don't want to die! Let me make up for lost time? Please?"

"Lost time? Is that how you've lived with yourself for all these years? You left two young female ChildForms to fend for themselves. Now here you're here asking for more than what you deserve?"

General Lyric realized her voice had risen. She closed her eyes, silently counting until she calmed down. She seldom lost her temper, but all of the suppressed emotions came flooding out of her at once. She hadn't realized how deeply her mother's abandonment had scarred her.

"I apologize for raising my voice to you, Mother. Just tell me this. Obviously you didn't marry King Dubian. Why did you never come for me?"

"I couldn't! I was banished to a place where no time, light, or love existed. The only thing I felt was the consistent burning of my flesh. Lyric, you don't know how terrible it was!" She rubbed her hands up and down her arms furiously. "I can still feel the Flames licking at my skin. The pain was unbearable!"

"You don't mean—were you in the Flames of Justice?!"

Lady Alarah nodded. "King Dubian had me beaten and thrown into them as punishment for upsetting Queen Opal."

General Lyric's mouth opened and closed. "How on Platirius did you escape?"

"I don't know. One minute I was in the Flames, and the next, I was in the wilderness. I don't know how I got there."

General Lyric's eyes narrowed. "The only Being who could've released you was Queen Vivant."

"Queen Vivant? She was a ChildForm the last time I saw her. A female is leading Platirius now?"

General Lyric nodded.

"I'm confident it wasn't her. But if she knows, won't she throw me back in?"

General Lyric sighed. "I don't know, but I can't keep this from her. She has to know you've been released. As the ruler of this queendom, it'll be up to her to decide what to do with you."

Lady Alarah rubbed her hands together. "Please, Lyric. Don't let me go back to the Flames! I lost my mind there." She threw herself on the general's lap. "I can't go back! I won't!"

General Lyric bent to untangle her arms from her legs. "You turned your back on your king and your planet. Do you actually think I'd follow in your footsteps? I'm not like you. My word is my honor. I won't betray Queen Vivant."

"Then I guess I'll have to await my fate. May I finish my supper? If I go back...food will be the last thing on my mind."

"Go right ahead," said General Lyric as she rose. "I expect to see you here when I return."

Lady Alarah looked at her like a ChildForm who'd just been caught pilfering cookies. "May I have another sandwich?"

She pointed at the platter of sandwiches. "There's plenty, Mother. Help yourself."

She strolled out into the warm night, wondering what Queen Vivant would say. As disappointed as she was in her mother, she wasn't ready to let her go yet. She hoped her leader would show mercy.

"And you say you don't know how you got out of the Flames?" asked King Anemi.

"No, Your Majesty, I don't. I woke up in a strange place and somehow wandered here."

King Anemi's eyes narrowed. She was lying, of course, but until he discovered who was helping her, he wouldn't strike. Her release hadn't thwarted his plans. She was just what he needed to keep General Lyric out of his hair.

He had a feeling Lady Alarah was about to give her daughter much more than a warm, cozy family reunion. Quite the opposite. He rubbed his hands together.

I have bigger fish to fry.

"Until I decide what to do with you, you may stay here with Lyric." He stuck a finger in her face. "But I'll warn you, don't let me see you poking around my grounds. You aren't to travel any farther than this cottage. Is that clear?"

She winced. "Of course, My Queen. Thank you."

"I'll go make up one of the spare bedrooms," said General Lyric.

Just before King Anemi turned to leave, Lady Alarah said, "It's wonderful to see you again. You've grown to be so beautiful! The last time I saw you was at your mother's DeathCeremony."

King Anemi looked her up and down. "WomanForm, are you deranged? My mother was dead long before you were born!"

She stared at him, mouth agape, when he stormed out of the cottage.

"Dead? I watched Queen Dellah grow up. What on Platirius is going on?"

F awn had just finished seeing her last patient. She reached down and took off her shoes. Slipping her feet into a pair of comfortable slippers, she leaned back in the chair, sighing heavily. It had been a long day. She groaned when the overhead speaker buzzed.

"Yes? What is it?"

"Dr. Azini, I know you asked not to be disturbed, but a young artist is here. He says he's owed payment for a painting. He refuses to leave."

Fawn sat upright. "A painting?"

"Yes, Doctor. He said he forwarded it to you weeks ago."

Fawn cast a side eye at the painting of her father. It was still sitting in the corner where she'd left it.

Getting up to pour a cup of ginger tea, she said, "Send him in."

"Yes, Dr. Azini."

The MaleForm entered just as Fawn added two lumps of sugar into the cup. He was tall with dark hair and eyes, and smooth olive skin.

"I'm sorry, I must be in the wrong office. I was told Dr. Azini was a MaleForm," he said.

"My father passed away a while ago. I'm running this institute now. My assistant said you haven't been compensated for a painting?"

He nodded. "That's right. Several months ago, King Belial asked me to paint Dr. Azini, so I did. He said the doctor would pay me personally after I shipped it out. I've been traveling, so I lost track of it. When I didn't hear anything, I decided to come here."

"How much did King Belial commission the painting for?"

She felt woozy after he quoted the amount. It would take months to save that amount of funds.

"Consider it done," said King Justin.

Fawn craned her neck around the artist and stood. "Your Highness! This is a surprise. I wasn't expecting you."

He shrugged. "I came to see if you'd cleaned out my old office. I've been itching to get back to practicing."

Her doubtful expression told him that wasn't going to happen.

"No?"

"Uh..."

"Well, let's discuss it after I take care of Mister... What did you say your name was?"

"Luis Perez," said the artist.

"Alright, Mr. Perez. Are you ready?"

"Yes, Your Highness."

King Justin raised his palm and transmitted the funds to him.

"Ah! You provided a very generous tip! Thank you, King Justin."

"No problem. Just one more thing? Take the painting with you. You can destroy it if you like, but Dr. Azini doesn't need it."

Luis looked from the king to Fawn, then at the painting. "Uh...sure. I'll get rid of it right now."

"Thank you, Mr. Perez."

"No problem," said Luis.

Fawn didn't realize she was holding her breath until Luis left.

King Justin gave her a teasing smile. "You know, a little birdie told me my subjects aren't allowed to say no to me."

"King Justin…"

"Would it really be a conflict of interest if I returned to work?"

She nodded. "A big one! I don't know how I'd live it down once it got around the galaxy that our king was working here."

"Wasn't King Noham a physician?"

"Yes, but once he took the throne, he stopped practicing. It's kind of a given. No one expects their king to look down their throat and tell them to say ahhhh."

He laughed. "Ah, alright! You drive a hard bargain, Dr. Azini. Well, if you won't let me come back to work, at least have lunch with me."

"That isn't allowed either."

He pointed at her. "Not true! Gallium told me my great-grandfather and grandmother used to break bread with their subjects at every meal. It brought them closer together as a kingdom. I personally love the idea."

"Well, that was a long time ago. Things were different back then. The security measures we have in place would take years to unravel. For your safety, it's best to leave them in place, My King. If you don't mind me saying so."

He crossed his foot over the other. "Does that go for personal lunches too?"

Her hands went to her curvaceous hips. "You don't want anyone to think you're showing favoritism," she said.

He cocked his head. "And if they do? What will happen?"

"Absolutely nothing," she admitted. "You're the king."

He slapped his hands together. "Good. I had a feeling you wouldn't come out for lunch, so I ordered two specials to go. They should be arriving about—"

"Hello, Your Highness!" said Phylicia Roundtree, a dining staff, bustling through the door. "I ran as fast as I could to get the food here. It's still piping hot."

"Well, thank you, but there was no need. We have warmers here."

Phylicia stared up at him. "I've lived on JanIus all my life and have seen several generations take the throne. None of them were ever served cold food and never will be."

He took the containers and cups from her. "Thank you very much. For the food and the fast service."

"You're welcome, King Justin." She tossed a curious glance at Fawn before she hurried off.

Closing the door with his foot, he said, "Now, let's see what we have."

Chapter 5

"My King, did you see the way she looked at me. This will be all over JanIus!"

"No, it won't," he said confidently. "I enacted my grandmother's gossip decree after we returned from Platirius. She won't say a word. Now have a seat, Dr. Azini. I heard you saw twenty patients today with no breaks. No argument!"

"I wouldn't dream of arguing with you."

"Now that's something I'm looking forward to."

He tapped the top of one of the containers. "Open it and tell me if you like it. If not, I'll trade mine with you."

She sighed with satisfaction when the warm steam and delicious aromas hit her nostrils. The deep plum carton held two crispy pork cutlets over cornbread dressing, mustard greens with pieces of smoked turkey, and potato salad. King Justin was ready to enjoy two slabs of beef ribs, pasta in a thick, creamy cheese sauce, and candied sweet potatoes.

"There's nothing better than sweet PotterBerry juice," he said.

"I can't thank you enough for this, Your Highness."

"Well, it's the least I can do after everything you've done for me. Now eat up! That's an order!"

She saluted him and laughed. It surprised him to discover he enjoyed hearing her laugh. He made a mental note to make her smile more often.

"So, how's General Lyric?"

"I haven't spoken with her for a couple of days. She's been really busy training the new recruits. I'll check in with her later this evening."

"I hope she's doing well," said Fawn.

She genuinely meant it. She held no animosity toward the king's lady, but she wasn't a fool. Beings who got on his mother's bad side ended up dead—one way or another. If Queen Revari wanted the general away from the king, then she'd move Heaven and Earth to make it happen. Fawn had a strange feeling that things were about to get worse for General Lyric. A lot worse.

L ady Alarah fell into a comfortable routine, wielding something she'd been good at all of her life: deception.

If Lyric wants a good mother, then that's what I'll become.

It worked. She prepared elaborate meals and kept the modest cottage spotless. In less time than she'd planned, they'd settled into a comfortable arrangement. General Lyric finally had what she'd always dreamed of—a loving mother.

Yet, at times, a dream can be nothing more than a ruse. If the dreamer doesn't wake up, they may be destined to wander aimlessly through mendacity, never fully coping with reality.

General Lyric had just finished briefing the latest recruits on how to properly sanitize and store their gear when her TeleScreen buzzed.

"Hello, I was wondering if I could speak with my beautiful lady? I haven't seen her in a couple of weeks and it's making me antsy."

"Justin! Oh, I'm so happy to hear from you! It's been so hectic around here."

"Well let me make things easier. Let me fly you out to JanIus for dinner."

Reaching the door of her cottage, she chewed on her bottom lip. "Hm. I have a better idea. Why don't you come here for supper? I have a surprise for you."

"To Platirius? Are you forgetting what happens when I'm on the grounds?"

"My cottage isn't on Platirius, it's on the outskirts. You'll be safe from the creepy ghosts. On my honor."

"Then how could I resist? Give me the coordinates and I'll be there around suppertime. Oh, and, Lyric? Can you wear that iris dress I bought you? I've been dying to see you in it."

She hesitated.

"What's the matter?"

"It's a bit sexy."

"I know. That's why I chose it. But if you're uncomfortable wearing it, I understand."

"No, it's just—well—you'll see when you get here."

Perplexed, King Justin blinked. "Okay. I'll see you soon. In a while!"

"In a while!"

"Are you going somewhere, My King?" asked Colonel Lionus.

"Yes, I'm having supper with my lady tonight."

"I'll have the pilot make preparations."

"Oh, no need. I can fly my own craft."

Colonel Lionus looked as if he wanted to say more, but didn't.

"What is it, Colonel? Let me guess, kings don't fly crafts?"

"They do, but not without soldiers. It makes you open to an ambush. Forgive me for saying it, Your Highness, but no one is more vulnerable to an attack than you."

"Because I'm half Human."

It was a statement, not a question, but Colonel Lionus nodded.

"The whole galaxy has been talking. A lot of Beings are against you ruling a realm."

"And what about you? How do you feel about it?"

"When I first learned about you, I felt the same. But as I've grown to know you, you remind me of King Carlomon. It's like having him back with us again."

The colonel bowed his head, then quickly raised it. "I'm ashamed to admit I was prejudiced against Humans. Watching you in action showed me how wrong I was."

King Justin motioned for him to take a seat in front of him.

"You genuinely care what happens to us. You don't put on airs. You even humbled yourself to listen when General Barrios taught you to defend yourself. You're nothing like King Dubian."

The colonel's hands remained open while he talked, an unspoken sign of trustworthiness.

"No matter what anyone says, I'm proud to have you as my king. And I'll defend you with my life."

King Justin fist bumped the colonel and stood up. "It means a lot to hear you say that. I've only met King Carlomon briefly, but I feel his spirit every day. He was a good and honorable king, and I intend to make him proud."

Colonel Lionus smiled. "I think you've already done it, Your Highness. Should I get the craft ready? Sorry, but we can't let you go anywhere alone."

King Justin sighed. "Alright. As long as you stay out of sight. It's been a long time since I've seen her, if you know what I mean."

A twinkle shone in the colonel's eye. "Oh yes, My King. I've been there a time or two!"

The TeleShield chimed softly when King Justin scanned his hand over it. Clutching two large bouquets of white roses, he tugged on the collar of his shirt. He didn't know why he was acting like it was his first time going to the prom.

General Lyric answered the door, dressed in a dusty-rose top and cream trousers.

I guess I won't be seeing the dress, he thought.

"I'm sorry, Justin. I know I put it in my wardrobe, but when I went to grab it, I couldn't find it!"

"It's okay," he said kissing her. "You look amazing in anything. Here, these are for you!"

"Oh, they're so beautiful! Come on in and I'll put them in some water."

A WomanForm was putting a large pot on the table. When she looked up at him and smiled, a chill went through him. Gallium had described her to him well enough to know she was—

"Justin, I'd like you to meet my mother, Lady Alarah of Coldarius."

King Justin took in her sharp blue-green eyes, regal nose, thin lips, and pale skin. She was several shades lighter than her daughter. A crooked scar ran across her right cheek.

He fought to find his voice. "It's a pleasure to meet you, Lady Alarah."

He almost bowed, but caught himself.

Lady Alarah chuckled. "You've been trained well. It's against propriety for royalty to bow to a commoner."

Trained?

"It's even more offensive to suggest royals need to be trained like animals," said King Justin.

General Lyric stopped smiling. "Justin! Mother taught etiquette classes when I was little. She meant no disrespect."

"Of course not," said Lady Alarah. "But Lyric, should you be addressing him by his first name?"

"Lyric and I don't use titles with each other," said Justin.

"You should, Lyric. It's improper to address a king so intimately. You may share his bed, but you're not his wife. Even the best bed wenches know their places."

"Lyric isn't my whore!"

"I never suggested she was, Your Highness," Lady Alarah smoothly interjected. "But you haven't made my daughter your wife. Therefore, as a commoner, she doesn't have the right to be so free with her tongue."

"She's the general of my aunt's army. I'd hardly consider that common."

"Yes, but she wasn't born into royalty. The rules of the galaxy are set in stone, King Justin."

"That didn't stop you from breaking a lot of them."

"King Justin," said General Lyric. "She's my mother. Please."

"No, Lyric, he's right. I didn't appreciate the life I had, and I hurt a lot of Beings. Spending many years in the Flames of

94

Justice has taught me to see the error of my ways. Thank you for correcting me, King Justin."

He stared at Lady Alarah, overwhelmed by a dark and foreboding feeling he couldn't comprehend.

"I want all of us to get off to a good start," said General Lyric. "King Justin—"

He turned to her. "You can't be serious—"

"King Justin," she firmly repeated. "My mother has paid for her crimes. You should know Queen Vivant has granted her permission to stay with me."

That surprised him. The last time he'd seen his aunt, she'd agreed that Lady Alarah wouldn't be set free. He decided to let it go. He didn't rule Platirius—she did. Whatever she decreed in her realm was her business. General Lyric was his.

"Let's agree to keep the formalities we had before in place, alright?"

His lips thinned. He hadn't known Lady Alarah for five minutes and already she was setting the tone for his relationship.

"Whatever you want, Lyric," he said.

General Lyric clapped her hands together once. "Good! Let's sit down and eat before the food gets cold. Mother has prepared a good spread!"

He washed his hands and sat down. Immediately, he noticed a fancy beet salad. His eyes silently met General Lyric's.

"Mother! I told you, Ju—the king is allergic to beets!"

"Oh! Oh my, I'm so sorry! I thought you said they were his favorite. And I spent a half-hour span making it look perfect!"

Lady Alarah stood up and grabbed the platter. "Don't worry, Your Highness. I'll get this out of your way!"

King Justin nodded toward a large blue crock. "What's in the pot?"

"Beef borscht," said Lady Alarah.

He kept his face impassive.

"But don't worry!" Lady Alarah assured him. "We have beef bourguignon with baby potatoes, an arugula salad with a lemon and thyme vinaigrette, and I baked a couple of loaves of crusty bread."

Her bright smile waned. "The appetizers were my only mistakes. I'm truly sorry about that! I was so nervous when Lyric told me we were having a king for dinner!"

General Lyric took her hand. "It's alright, Mother. Everything looks delicious. King Justin is very kind. He's not holding anything against you." She looked at him. "Everything is fine now."

None of it was fine with him. He was seething, but he knew better than to show it in front of them.

"I agree with Lyric," he said. "It looks as if you've spent a lot of time preparing this. I'm sure we'll all enjoy it."

Taking General Lyric's hand in his, he noted a hint of disdain in Lady Alarah's eyes. Remembering she was Coldarian, he kept his mind clear so she couldn't read his thoughts.

The meal was eaten primarily in silence while General Lyric tried to keep conversation flowing between them. Lady Alarah, however, had barely said two words to him.

"If you think I'm being rude, Your Highness, I'm not. I have a thousand questions, but all of them would be improper to ask a royal."

"Ask away. I have nothing to hide."

"No, I don't think that would be proper. Maybe next time."

In his heart, he felt she'd made the beet dishes on purpose. He also suspected that if the general's mother had her way, there wouldn't be a next time. By the time dessert was served, an apple gratin, he was ready to leave.

Lady Alarah had a way of speaking that bordered on insulting, but was just passive enough to make one appear to be overreacting if they called her out on it. After consuming a slice of pie and coffee, he wiped his mouth and pushed back his chair.

"General Lyric, would you like to escort me out?"

Lady Alarah gave him a false smile. "I don't remember when I've enjoyed a meal more than this. Thank you so much for coming, King Justin. You've made my daughter very happy."

"Thank you for having me. Take care of yourself."

They held hands as they walked down the short path to his craft.

"I know you two got off to a rocky start, but please give her a chance, King Justin? I know once you get to know her, you'll like her!"

"Will you stop with that king nonsense?" he snapped. "Are we going to give each other titles in bed too?"

She dropped his hand. "There's no reason to be mean about it! Maybe we aren't as far enough from Platirius as I thought."

He suspected she was right. On more than one occasion, he'd suppressed the urge to reach across the table and strangle her mother. It had deeply shaken him. He'd never wanted to raise his hand to a female since he'd held King Dubian's BrainStaff.

"Maybe you should come to JanIus next time. It'll be...less crowded."

She clasped her hands together, staring down at her feet. "I can't leave Mother alone."

"Are you serious? Lyric, she's not a ChildForm! What do you do with her when you're working?"

"That's different. We're all here together. She's good at keeping her own company, but I'd worry about her if I were gone for too long."

"We spend weekends together, not months," he countered.

She raised her hands in surrender. "I don't want to argue with you. I finally have one of my ParentForms back. Can't you be happy for me?"

"I'm thrilled for you, but we already don't spend enough time together. I knew coming into the game I'd play second fiddle to your job, but I feel like I'm in third place now that your mother is here! Where's my place in your life, Lyric? Do I matter to you at all?"

"You know you do."

"Do I? Tell me. When will I see you again?"

Her silence told him he wasn't imagining things. He held up one finger followed by another. "Your career, and now, your mother. Let me ask you again, where do I fit in?"

"You're the first MaleForm I've held inside my body. Isn't that enough to know how much I care about you?"

He shook his head and looked up at the stars. They seemed happier than he was at the moment. "Okay. I'll wait until you're free."

She stood on the tip of her toes and kissed him. "Thank you."

He nodded toward the cottage. "You should get back home."

Sexually frustrated and mentally drained, he turned toward his craft and left her standing there. Lady Alarah watched them from the window, crushing the soft petals of a rose in her hand.

Six months later

King Justin threw a heavy jardiniere against the wall. It crashed just a few feet from Fawn.

"Whoa! Did I come at a bad time? What's going on, Your Highness?"

"Sorry. None of it hit you, did it?"

"No, but I feel sorry for the wall. I've never known you to have a temper. Is it my place to ask what's wrong?"

"Of course it is, and I wish everyone would stop treating me like I'm—"

She grinned at him. "Like what? Royalty?"

"I had no choice in becoming a king, but I shouldn't have to give up everyone I care about," he said glumly.

"You don't have to. We're still here. In time, you'll adjust to the new order."

"I gotta tell you, Fawn, I'm not good at it. I haven't seen Lyric in months. Every time we make a date, something comes up with her mother. It's driving me crazy!"

Fawn pursed her lips together and listened.

"And? If I call Lyric's home, her mother tells me she's sleeping or out with Queen Vivant. But that's not true. Just before she disconnected the transmission in the middle of my next question, Queen Vivant told me she rarely sees Lyric anymore. I can't go to Platirius, because when I do, I turn into a raving lunatic! It shouldn't be this hard to be with the one you love!"

He sighed. "You always have good advice. What should I do?"

"I'm afraid I can't help you on this. I'm sorry, My King."

He shook his head. "I guess I should face that it's over. I've been holding my breath waiting for her to tell me to go. And I'm too proud to tell her I've had enough of her mother's antics. I don't like admitting when I've lost."

She wanted to hold him, but it was forbidden. "I came to bring you these from the dining chamber. It's a box of your favorite white chocolate-hazelnut cookies. I hope they'll cheer you up."

He took the box from her. "You always think of me. Thank you."

She shrugged. "And I always will! I'll see you in a while, My King."

"In a while," he said absently.

Fawn turned and pitched forward into darkness. The last thing she heard was her king screaming her name.

"Thank you for getting her here so fast, King Justin," said Dr. Corning. "I'm afraid it's not good news. It's a glioblastoma."

King Justin closed his eyes, inhaling sharply. *No. God, please no!*

"You're the only neurosurgeon JanIus has, but now that you're king, performing the operation is out of the question. It would be a huge conflict of interest. I've sent news to Queen Revari. We're hoping she'll help her."

"My mother? Why would she help Fawn?"

"Queen Revari specifically informed us if anything happened, we were to notify her at once. Especially about Dr. Azini."

His curiosity piqued, the king asked, "Why? What's her interest in Fawn?"

"I don't know, but it appears the queen is quite fond of her. She's visited her several times."

"Without coming to see me? That's odd."

Dr. Corning shrugged. "Maybe not. WomenForms can form the strangest bonds. I don't know if you know, but Dr. Azini was handpicked by Queen Revari for the ParaNurture program."

He knew, but what went on between royals was none of Dr. Corning's business.

"It doesn't matter what she told you. I run JanIus, not her."

"Y–yes course, Your Highness!" stammered Dr. Corning.

"I want to see the CT scans of Fawn's brain to ascertain the location of the tumor. Sooner than later, Doctor."

"Yes, My King!"

After reviewing the tests and bloodwork, King Justin summoned Dr. Corning.

"It's a small tumor positioned on her cerebrum. Thankfully, it hasn't invaded any of her surrounding brain tissue. Our intraoperative MRI is more advanced than the technology I worked with on Earth. It can help achieve the best possible outcome in craniotomy. I'm confident I can get it all so she won't need chemotherapy. By all accounts, the chances of it returning are less than 30%."

"That's wonderful! Dr. Azini is going to be alright! Praise The One!"

His TeleScreen beeped.

Mother.

"Yes, Queen Revari?"

She frowned. "What's going on with Dr. Azini? I want her shipped here immediately."

He held up a hand. "I'm taking care of it, Mama."

"You're going to operate on her? Why?"

"Because I'm the best at what I do," he said sharply.

"Don't take that tone with me. I know how good you are, but Revani has skilled physicians who can help her too."

"They're not better than me," he said confidently. "I respect your opinion and I have no doubt you have a skilled medical team. But I'm not trusting any other surgeon with Fawn's life. There's no argument on this—I'm doing the surgery."

Queen Revari sat back in the chair, hiding a smile. "Very well. Let me know if you need more staff. I'm flying out to JanIus. I should be there by morning."

"Why?"

"Fawn's mother is a disgrace. She can't even stay sober enough to support her daughter during this difficult time. I'm willing to step in to do what she can't."

"What is your interest in Fawn?"

"I like her," she said. "I think she's a wonderful WomanForm. And, she's what I could've been had my mother lived." Her eyes narrowed. "You may be a king, but you're not my boss! I'll be at her side when she comes out of surgery."

He looked toward the heavens. "Do you ever stop being so intense?"

She crossed one knee over the other. "No."

"Okay. I know I won't win this one, so I won't even try. You're right. Fawn needs all the support she can get right now."

"Yes, she does. And she deserves it. I've always wanted a daughter like Fawn."

King Justin smiled. "She's quite a Being."

Intrigued by his soft tone, Queen Revari smiled. "I'm glad you're noticing her qualities."

"I've always noticed them. From the very first day I met her. Oh! Gallium says you have a lot of paintings of Dad. Do you mind if I have one?"

"Of course not. I'll bring several and have them hung in your palace."

"I'll put them in my bedroom. Don't get me wrong, I'm not ashamed of my father. I just don't want anyone pointing at him or whispering."

"No one would dare," she said confidently. "As you wish. I'll bring them tomorrow."

"Thank you, Mama."

"You're welcome. And thank you for helping Fawn."

"Nothing would bring me more pleasure than to see her up and moving about again. I don't know what I'd do if I couldn't look into her eyes again."

"In a while, son."

"In a while, Mother."

Queen Revari disconnected the transmission and kicked her feet in the air like a ChildForm. Although her son had no idea what he'd just admitted to, she did. A mother always knows.

K ing Anemi entered the secret research chamber under Platirius. He was grateful his idiotic son hadn't discovered it when he'd torn down the chambers that had stood since his father passed the throne to him.

A MaleForm sat in a high-powered chair.

Gazing at him, the king said, "The time has come for you to seek out my enemies. I don't need to tell you what will happen if you fail me."

Bracing both arms on the chair, he leaned forward, staring into the MaleForm's face.

"What is your name?" asked King Anemi.

The MaleForm opened his eyes. "I am General Lucian Kron."

T he princesses sat nervously before King Anemi, wondering why they had been summoned.

Tossing them a bored look, he said, "I've arranged for all of you to be married. You'll have a single ceremony and afterward will go to three different planets with your husbands. I'll hold on to the funds King Micah willed to you until you reach the proper age."

"What?" asked Princess Tyre.

"Mother!" cried Princess Teenah. "You said we could marry whom we love!"

Princess Tarah stared hard at him.

"Love? Nonsense," said King Anemi. "Arranged marriages have existed on Platirius before even my father's time."

The princesses looked at each other.

"But Grandfather Dubian and Grandmother Dellah's marriage wasn't arranged," said Princess Tyre. "They—"

"Silence!" he roared. "Don't mention Dubian's name in my presence!"

Everyone stared at him as if he'd lost his mind.

"Now, where was I? Ah! The kings I've selected for you are willing to give me fifty percent interest in their kingdoms. This will be one of my most profitable investments to date."

His focus shifted to Princess Tarah. "It looks as if you're glaring at me again. That would be a mistake."

Colonel Kourtney's head snapped up. She and Sergeant Alicia shared a shocked glance. The queen had never spoken to her daughters that way.

Princess Tarah held his gaze. "Something's wrong. You've always been in control of your emotions, but you didn't shed a tear at Grandfather's DeathCeremony. You didn't bother to comfort Grandmother either."

The king spread his hands wide. "Comfort her? Is she not a grown WomanForm capable of tending to her own needs? What do you take me for? A NurseForm?"

"I don't know what you are," snapped Princess Tarah. "But whatever it is, it's beneath a queen!"

In a rage, King Anemi bolted up, towering over the princesses. "One more word and I'll make sure you take your vows today! Is that clear?"

Sergeant Alicia's stoic facade morphed into puzzlement.

Doesn't the queen always say, "Have I been heard?"

Kneeling to Princess Tarah, he looked her in the eye and said, "No spoiled princess will speak to me as if I don't own panties on her pampered ass!"

Princess Tyre and Teenah were holding onto each of their sister's arms, staring at their mother as if they'd never seen her before. Silent, angry tears rolled down Princess Tarah's face. Enraged silver eyes met sullen gray ones.

"Yes?" goaded King Anemi. "Do you have something else you'd like to say to me?"

Defeated, Princess Tarah lowered her head.

"That's better," said King Anemi, standing straight again. "I've grown weary of taking care of three AdultForms. You eat my food and laugh loudly in my halls. You don't make financial contributions to my realm, so what's the point of keeping you around?"

Walking around the desk to take a seat, he said, "Your husbands will be King Amos, King Hosiah, and King Saul."

"But they're the oldest kings in the galaxy!" said Princess Teenah. "And they're stinky!"

"It's no worse than the stench of WomenForms crowding my halls. The sooner I get rid of you, the sooner things can return to the way they were."

Captain Kourtney's eyes narrowed. *Were they not all WomenForms?*

The queen sounded like a MaleForm, and a misogynistic one at that. For weeks, she'd observed Queen Vivant's behavior. She hadn't been herself since they'd won against King Belial. Could his dark magic have lasted after his death? She didn't know. But she knew someone who would.

Chapter 6

"She's been avoiding me for weeks," said Advisor TamRi. "Every time I try to set up a meeting with her, she postpones it."

"She just yelled at the princesses in front of Sergeant Alicia and I," said Captain Kourtney.

Advisor TamRi stopped monitoring the surveillance footage and turned to her. "I can't imagine the queen being verbally abusive to her daughters."

"It's true," said Sergeant Alicia. "And the princesses said she showed no emotion at King Micah's funeral. They said it seemed as if she were glad he was dead."

"Well, she's always been stoic. We know that. We also know she adored King Micah." Advisor TamRi sat thinking. "Something isn't right."

"I agree, Advisor, and we have to figure it out before she marries off the princesses," said Captain Kourtney.

Advisor TamRi spun her chair from the elaborate surveillance system. "Before she what?"

When the TeleShield buzzed, Major Sonee and Sergeant Thea entered with General Lyric.

"Okay, so the Vivacians are all here now," said Captain Kourtney. "Something is wrong with the queen. Have any of you seen her acting strangely or out of character?"

General Lyric chewed on her bottom lip. "Well, I noticed she was sitting on the balcony with no undergarments. When I pointed it out, she asked if she should shave her vagina. And...another Being said something strange too. She said she remembered seeing her at Queen Dellah's DeathCeremony, but the queen told her that her mother had passed before she was born."

"According to the records, Queen Dellah was laid to rest on Coldarius," said Advisor TamRi. "Other than you, Gallium, and General Legend, who would remember that?"

General Lyric cleared her throat. "I can't give the Being's identity, but I believe them."

"Alright, has anyone else noticed something strange?" asked Advisor TamRi.

"I saw her sitting on the throne like a MaleForm," said Sergeant Thea. "Her legs were spread wide open."

"I was present when she berated a dining staff yesterday for not serving carrot puree at supper," said Sergeant Alicia. "She loves vegetables, but not carrots. I've never seen her eat them."

"What on Platirius is happening?" asked Advisor TamRi.

"We need to keep tabs on her like we did when she was using Callidut," said General Lyric. "But we can't let her know we're watching her. I've compiled a list of all the odd things she's done since our last battle."

She leaned against a block of surveillance monitors. "After we've observed her for a while, we'll put our heads together and compare notes again. And above all, she should never be left alone with the princesses. We can't let them marry those decrepit, disgusting kings. It's our job to protect them—even from their mother."

While the Vivacians devised a plan, the princesses decided to take control of the situation. They didn't notice a craft speeding away from Platirius. Princess Tarah sat at the controls with her sisters sitting behind her.

"No one will force us to marry dirty old kings! Not even you, Mother!"

After six hours, King Justin sat back and put down his scalpel. A NurseForm wiped the beads of sweat on his forehead.

"It's done," he said wearily. "I removed all of the tumor. Dr. Azini will be fine."

Dr. Chirp, Dr. Clint, and NurseForms cheered.

"After you get her sewn up, we'll move her into a recovery room," said Dr. Chirp.

"No," said King Justin. "I had a room prepared for her inside the palace. She's to be transported where I can keep an eye on her. I've already ordered some of my nursing staff to notify me of her condition every half-hour."

"Yes, King Justin," said a NurseForm. "We'll get it done."

He rolled his neck. He was exhausted, but the worst was over. Knowing Fawn had a good chance of surviving made his heart soar.

Queen Revari was waiting for him outside the surgery chamber with General Legend. "How is she? And how are you, son? You look worn out."

"JanIus's technology is far more advanced than I realized! It made the surgery easier, but it took a lot out of me. I had to stay on top of the mechanisms without losing focus. Fawn will be just fine. They're moving her to the palace now."

General Legend clapped her hands together. "That's wonderful news!"

Bracing both hands behind his neck, he said, "I need a shower and a short nap. I want to be alert when she wakes up."

"She may not awaken until tomorrow. Why don't you take some time to rest? You have dozens of NurseForms to see to her needs, and Legend and I are here too. I had the paintings of your father hung in your bed chamber."

Grateful to have supportive family, he hugged them. "I don't know what I'd do without you. Thank you, Mama."

Queen Revari gave him a pat on the shoulder. "That's what we're here for."

"Well, come on. Let us go!" said General Legend. "I want to see how fabulous her bed chamber looks!"

"You two go ahead. I'll be right behind you," said Queen Revari.

She waited until they were out of sight before turning to an approaching NurseForm.

She read her name tag. "Rose Pratt. My son told me the surgery was a success. Is there anything else I should know?"

A chart trembled in Rose's hands. "Nothing concerning Dr. Azini. We're all committed to taking good care of her, My Queen. But you should know the princesses are here."

Queen Revari rolled her eyes. "That's nothing new. They've become obsessed with partying."

"They seemed very upset, Your Highness. They asked for the king, but he was performing Dr. Azini's surgery. One of the soldiers escorted them to the palace to wait for him."

"He needs rest. Whatever they have going on will have to wait. In the meantime, your top priority is making sure Dr. Azini has a full recovery. Have I been heard, NurseForm Pratt?"

"Yes, Queen Revari!"

She watched Rose hurry off.

It's the daytime. The princesses don't visit JanIus until after hours. What's so urgent that they came here to see Justin?

She picked up the pace on her way to the palace, determined to find out.

K ing Justin had fallen into a deep sleep.

He saw Fawn standing in the middle of a dance hall. Her flowing white gown bloomed around her ankles.

He took her hand and kissed it. "May I have this dance?" he asked.

Smiling up at him, she took his hand as he whirled her around the floor, with hundreds of faceless spectators looking on.

He smiled down at her, becoming lost in her beautiful golden-brown eyes. Suddenly, the doors flew open. Queen Vivant entered holding an Azgoate.

"Isn't this a lovely sight?" she asked, aiming the weapon at Fawn's head.

He tried to shield Fawn's body with his, but his reflexes were slower than usual. The sharp blast sounded from the Azgoate and hit home, separating Fawn's brain from her skull. Shouting her name, he reached for her and missed. When she fell, he felt JanIus explode, then speed toward Platirius.

Fawn's corpse opened its eyes. "We're merging with Hell," it said.

His father stood between the planets, his sad eyes boring into his. Blood gushed from a head wound and pooled at his feet.

"Platirius is evil, son."

Oliver Ascencio pulled back his scalp, revealing a gaping hole where his brain should've been. "Look what they did to me."

The spirits of the old kings entered King Justin, hungry for revenge.

King Anemi's voice was louder than the colliding planets. "Kill them all!"

"Noooooooooooo!" shouted King Justin.

He bolted awake and sat up in bed, panting harshly. Willing himself to control his breathing, his frantic eyes searched the dark bed chamber. His father's face, illuminated by the moon's rays, smiled down at him in the darkness. That comforted him. Wiping the sweat from his face, he lay back against the mattress, staring through the transparent ceiling at the fading stars until the sun rose.

Fawn!

Quickly jumping out of bed, he rushed into the bath chamber to shower. He wanted to be at her side when she woke up. Donning a fresh change of clothes, he groomed his hair and dashed on a bit of cologne. A dining staff caught up with his long strides as he headed to see Fawn.

"Good morning, Your Majesty! Queen Revari ordered us to have your breakfast ready when you awakened. Should we set it on the table now?"

"Hello, Tiye. No, I'm not ready to eat yet. I have to see Fawn first."

She bowed to him. "Of course, Your Highness. It'll be ready when you're done."

"Thank you, Tiye."

He entered Fawn's bed chamber, standing still for a moment. Her soft curls were carefully arranged around a large patch of shaved scalp. Dozens of monitors surrounded her. The NurseForms stood and bowed to him when he approached her bed.

"Good morning, Your Highness. We've been taking Dr. Azini's vitals every two hours. She hasn't awakened yet, but we're expecting her to very soon."

"Thank you, NurseForm Adams."

He scanned over the notes that had been recorded since the surgery. Everything was going as it should. He sat down next to her, gently caressing her small hand. She looked so peaceful and beautiful. Softly gliding a thumb across the back of her hand, he sat silently, being careful not to disturb her rest.

"Should we have your breakfast brought in here, Your Highness? Queen Revari said she wanted you to eat immediately."

"No. I've already informed the dining staff of my plans. He paused for a moment. When he spoke again, his tone was still friendly, yet firm. "My mother doesn't rule JanIus. I do."

The NurseForms shared a nervous glance.

He looked up at them. "I understand who my mother is, but she's not your boss. No matter what she says, please listen to my orders, not hers."

The NurseForms bowed. "Yes, My King."

"Have you eaten yet?" he asked.

They looked at each other again. "No," said NurseForm Adams. "But we can't leave until we're relieved. It's Queen Revari's...orders."

King Justin sighed and sent a transmission on his TeleScreen.

"Please go and have breakfast. My mother should be here soon, so take the back door. I'll keep watch over Fawn until the other shift arrives. They should be here in about twenty minutes."

The NurseForms thanked him and bowed. Queen Revari entered minutes after they exited.

"You need me?" She looked at Fawn. "Has something happened to her?"

"No, but something is happening, and I don't like it. Please explain to me why my staff are acting as if this is Revani?"

She moved to the other side of Fawn, carefully pushing a lock of hair to the side. "General Legend did a beautiful job with her hair. I don't speak for your staff, Justin. Maybe you should ask them."

His eyes never left hers. "No, I think I'm asking the right one. Everyone except Gallium is terrified of you. That doesn't sit well with me."

She shrugged. "I am who I am. I can't help if Beings are intimidated by my presence."

"Mama, I'm going to make this plain: if you want to rule JanIus, you may do so with my blessing. I'll wait until Fawn partially recovers and transport her with me to Earth. When she's back to her old self again, it'll be her choice on whether she wants to return to JanIus or not. But as for me, you'll never see me again."

She waved at him. "You're making a big deal out of nothing, Justin! Am I not allowed to make sure you eat?"

"Don't gaslight me. I'm not a fool! You wouldn't have brought me to a planet where you didn't have some form of control. I refuse to be a king in your shadow. It's an insult to my manhood. So, either you back off and stop running JanIus, or this is where you and I get off. And trust me, I won't be returning to Space for a second time!"

"Your aunt and I have a controlling interest in JanIus. That's a far cry from running it."

He wasn't letting her off so easily.

"Since I stopped working at the institute, I've had a lot of time to think. King Leighton knew who I was from the beginning. He protected me because of you. You get off on controlling everyone and everything around you. I don't know if you treated my father the same, but you won't do it to me!"

"Oliver was very easy going, but I didn't involve myself in his business. He ran Blind Trust completely without my help."

"Who's running it now? I'm sure you didn't let it go, just like that."

"It was dissolved during the second year I was in the Chamber of Despair. There was nothing I could do to save it. Or him."

"And you think interfering in my life gives you power you didn't have back then. Whether you're willing to admit it or not, you're just as controlling as King Dubian."

Her eyes flashed dangerously, but he didn't back down.

"Had he left you alone, you would've been happy with my dad. But he didn't, and his meddling destroyed your life. Don't you see how that logic applies to me? If you allowed me to live my life my way, I would be happier."

"There's nothing I want more than your happiness. I don't want you to leave. This is your realm, not mine. I only asked the dining staff to have your breakfast ready. What's so wrong with that?"

"You don't ask. You give orders. It isn't the same."

"We are rulers, Justin. We don't exist to be friends with everyone. If you're too nice, some might take your kindness for weakness. You must be fair but firm with your subjects."

"Grandmother was kind to her subjects. No one tried it with her."

She smirked. "They knew better."

"I don't want to have this conversation with you again. And I won't. I'm asking you to let me lead JanIus my way."

"Done. Is there anything else?"

"Yes. Please be happy. I want you to find light and love too. What happened to my father was awful, but I don't think he'd want you to go the rest of your life closed off to finding someone who'll love you. Aunt Vivant has found it again. Love isn't wrong, Mama. Give yourself a chance."

"I don't want another MaleForm breathing on me," she said dismissively. "Now, if you want me to respect your wishes, I advise you to do the same."

"Fine. I won't interfere with your life if you give me the same courtesy."

She refrained from rolling her eyes. "Well, I'm glad we cleared that up. What did the princesses want with you?"

King Justin blinked. "I don't know. I haven't seen them in weeks."

Adjusting Fawn's blankets, she said, "They're here at the palace, looking for you."

"Fawn is my priority right now. I'll meet with them after I sit with her for a while. I don't want her to feel lonely. Perhaps we can all have breakfast together like we did on Revani. That was nice, wasn't it?"

She smiled. "Yes, it was." She looked down at Fawn. "And when Fawn gets better, she'll join us." Tossing him a mocking look, she asked, "Am I allowed to tell the dining staff we'll be having a family breakfast?"

He sighed. "Yes, Mama. Now, will you please leave us alone? I want to spend some time with her before I assume my duties for the day."

She saluted him. "Yes, King Justin. See you in a while."

"And thank you for the paintings. When I woke up today and saw Dad, I felt at peace. I could tell he was an amazing man."

"Yes, he was. The best."

He held Fawn's hand up to his face. "I need you to get better, Colonel. I never realized how much light you bring into my world or how my loneliness lifts when you're around. You were the first friend I made here."

Gently caressing her hand, he said, "I need you in my life, Fawn. More than you know."

Watching how tender he was with her made Queen Revari smile. She hoped Lady Alarah was doing her part. If not, there would be hell to pay.

General Lyric whistled softly while tidying up her bed chamber. After putting away a basket of laundry, something strange caught her eye. She approached the fireplace and kneeled. Since she seldom used it, she was surprised a fire had recently been lit.

A small piece of partially burned cloth lay in the corner. Picking it up, she realized it was a part of the dress King Justin had wanted her to wear when he came to dinner.

She burned my dress?! Why?

Noting a large pile of ashes, an uneasy feeling swept over her. Throwing open the doors to her walk-in closet, she brought a fist to her mouth. Everything King Justin had bought her was gone! She rushed to the drawers, quickly pulling them out to inspect their contents.

All of her perfume, jewelry, and trinkets were gone! Grabbing a poker, she sifted through the ashes. The remnants of a bracelet Queen Vivant had gifted to her had been burned. The ashes had a strong odor of roses. A single white petal had survived the flames.

She shook her head in disbelief. Everything came flooding back to her at once. The missed calls, the numerous times her mother had told her King Justin had broken their dates at the last minute. She hadn't seen him in almost a year. And her mother was to blame! Gallium's words came back to her.

She was haughty and vicious. She thought she was better than everyone else. And she made it her mission to make trouble for others.

"Serving beets to Justin wasn't a mistake. She did it on purpose," she whispered. Her head bowed, tears stinging her eyes. "Why would she do this to me?"

"Lyric! Oh, Lyric, you have to come quickly!"

General Lyric raised her head and stared at her, allowing her to see the hurt and rage in her eyes. "What is it, Mother?"

"It's your father! He's still alive! He's been found! Please, you have to take me to him!"

She struggled to make sense of it. "What? Mother, Gallium said Father died in a crash!"

"I don't care what he said! I have proof! He's alive, and we have to help him. Please take me to the mountains now! You don't know, but that used to be the border between Coldarius and Platirius! He's been there all this time. We have to go now—he needs us, Lyric!"

If there was the slightest chance her father was alive, she was willing to take it. She'd deal with her mother's treachery once she returned. She didn't want to ask her to leave, but she couldn't overlook what she'd done.

She realized Lady Alarah had been deceiving her from the moment she met her. All of the frustration and anxiety she'd lived with for months hadn't been her imagination. She only hoped her mother would have the dignity to leave her in peace.

The winds blowing through the mountains were harsh and unwelcoming. For nearly half an hour, she followed Lady Alarah down a dark path.

"Mother, who told you Father was here?"

"An old acquaintance of mine. He was surprised to see I was alive. I didn't have time to think. I just wanted to get here as fast as I could after he told me Iham hadn't died. I can't wait to see the look on your face when you see..."

Her voice trailed off.

"When I see what, Mother?"

"There!" said Lady Alarah, pointing to an old, large craft.

General Lyric gasped. "By The One! It looks like it's been here forever!"

They couldn't reach the craft from where they stood, but she could see it plainly. One side of the old, weather-beaten frame had been destroyed. Amazingly, the rest of it was intact. She recognized Platirius's crest on the door.

"How could Father have survived this? And where is he now?"

"He's there, Lyric," said Lady Alarah, pointing to something at the base of the mountain.

General Lyric looked down and screamed. "No!"

A skeleton lay among the tall grass. It was in perfect condition. Its empty eyes gaped at them with a smile only Death could finalize. A sinister gleam formed in Lady Alarah's eyes. For the first time, the general saw who her mother really was. An evil, opportunistic sociopath who enjoyed taking pleasure in the misery of others.

Examining the skeleton more carefully, she noted the weapons still affixed in his holster. Whirling to her mother, she said, "Why would you bring me here? That's a Platirian crest!"

Lady Alarah moved closer to her, wickedness blazing in her eyes. "Yes, so? Your father worked for King Dubian, did he not?"

She smiled at the general. "Don't you recognize your own father, Lyric?"

"I'd know him anywhere, but you're a different story. I don't think I've ever seen who you are until this moment." She pointed to the body. "That is a testament to who you are. Using pain—old or new—to destroy the lives of others!"

Lady Alarah sneered. "Destroyed? When have you ever been destroyed? When have you ever cut your teeth on Death's sword, daughter? Because of me, you've lived a charmed life being Queen Vivant's general and whoring yourself out to a king! You haven't thanked me once!"

General Lyric stared at her. "Thank you? For what? Interfering with my relationship? Messing with my head after I took you in, and now this? You know how I feel about my father! How could you do something so cruel?"

"Because I *know* how you feel about *him*!" shouted Lady Alarah. "You always loved him more than me! You doted on him and ignored me when I was the one who disfigured my body giving birth to you! You were an ungrateful brat then, and you still are!"

General Lyric shook her head slowly. "You are...a treacherous WomanForm. Absolutely soulless. You won't get away with this!"

She clucked her tongue. "My dearest Lyric. Who's going to tell?"

General Lyric felt her shove her hard in the chest. Losing her balance, she screamed as she fell backward, tumbling down the sharp, jagged cliff. She landed on her back next to the bones. Lady Alarah stared down at her for a long time, then left her lying there alone.

King Justin sat with the princesses, Queen Revari, General Legend, and Gallium at breakfast.

"She wants you to marry those old fools? I don't know her that well, but I can't see her doing that."

"It's true. She's been acting so strange lately," said Princess Tarah. "I know it sounds crazy, but it doesn't feel like Mother is with us. She feels like a stranger."

King Justin cut into his steak. "You can stay here for as long as you like. You're family and families should stick together. There's been enough in-fighting among us. Too much."

"She's not using again," said Queen Revari confidently. "Gallium and I made sure all of King Belial's Callidut was destroyed. "Maybe she's thinking of marrying King Asa and wants to clear out the palace."

"Mother wouldn't do that to us, Aunt Reve," said Princess Teenah.

"I wouldn't have believed she'd force you into marriage either, but here we are," said Queen Revari.

Princess Teenah blinked back tears while Princess Tyre patted her sister's shoulder. "I just hope she doesn't come for us and drag us home."

"I won't let that happen," said King Justin. "I'll try to make her see reason. As for wealth, Aunt Vivant has more of that than she knows what to do with. Her logic for wanting you to marry doesn't make any sense."

"I agree," said General Legend. "Queen Vivant and I have never gotten along, but I know she loves the three of you more than her life. We'll find out what's going on."

Queen Revari's TeleScreen chimed. Scanning the caller's information, she said, "I have to take this."

She stepped out into the gardens, making sure the coast was clear before she spoke. "What is it? You'd better have a damn good reason for bothering me!"

"It's done," said Lady Alarah.

"*What* is done? Do you realize you're interrupting me spending time with my son?"

"Unfortunately, time is something my daughter has run out of. Lyric is dead. I pushed her off a cliff and left her. The field where she is has been abandoned for years. No one will find the body."

Queen Revari looked at her in disbelief. "You murdered your own ChildForm? By The One, you're the epitome of wickedness. I told you to break up her and my son's relationship. I never ordered you to kill her."

"Forgive me, My Queen, but you said to get rid of her. So I did."

"She's your daughter. Don't you feel the slightest bit of remorse?"

Lady Alarah shrugged. "I performed a job for Her Majesty—nothing more. May I please have my payment now?"

Queen Revari clenched her teeth. "Listen, you murdered her for yourself, not me! It would be wise for you to keep that in mind. Your funds will be sent to you within the hour."

She never liked General Lyric, but Lady Alarah's actions sickened her.

"I'm showing you a kindness by letting you live, but never show your face again. If you do, I'll slit your throat twice!"

"Yes, Your Majesty. I understand."

Queen Revari disconnected the transmission. *General Lyric is dead.* "Well, that's something I didn't see coming."

Her mind whirling fast, she returned to the dining hall and added another stack of pancakes to her plate.

Lady Alarah doesn't deserve to live for what she's done. I'll let her think she got away with it, then I'll kill her.

She looked over at King Justin, who was talking with Gallium.

My son can never know the part I played in this. She may not mind losing her daughter, but I won't watch my son walk out of my life again. Not ever.

K ing Justin tried to keep his mind off Fawn, but it was difficult. He wanted to hear her voice so badly, it was killing him.

"King Justin! King Justin!"

He turned around and saw the triplets running over to him.

"Hey, guys! Tio, Tyer, and Tautumn! What's up?"

"Hi, King Justin! I think it's really cool you're our king now!" said Tio. "I liked King Leighton too, but I like you being in charge too!"

King Justin ruffled his hair. "Thank you, Tio. That means a lot to me."

He surveyed the trio. "How are things with the Overmills?"

"We miss our father a lot, but they've been really good to us," said Tautumn. "I hope nothing happens to them."

King Justin cocked his head. "Why would something happen to them?"

Tautumn shrugged. "I don't know. I just don't want to get comfortable and something bad happens again."

"You can't live life that way. You have to let go and trust that The One knows best for us. Bad things happen, but trouble doesn't last always. There's no expiration date on grief either."

He kneeled to their level. "You're allowed to grieve for your father for as long as you need to. Remember the happy times too. That's how we keep our loved ones with us forever."

Tautumn nodded. "We will. Thanks, King Justin. Let us go!"

King Justin watched them run off. He, too, had grieved for his adoptive father at their age. No one knew how the brothers felt more than he.

"My King!" said a NurseForm. "Dr. Azini is awake!"

He shot up like a rocket, running faster than he'd ever run in his life.

Chapter 7

King Jonah flew his craft over the large fields, circling back to inspect the acres of land carefully. His surveillance team had pinpointed the location where the video footage shown at King Micah's DeathCeremony had been taken. After searching for an hour, he was about to peruse another part of the land when he spotted something. When he lowered the craft, the object came into view.

"It's a craft!" said Sergeant Honing.

"Can you see the seal?"

"Not at this height, My King."

"Then we need to get closer," said King Jonah.

Sergeant Honing took off his headphones and pointed at the ground.

"Look there, Your Highness! It's a WomanForm! She's lying next to the craft!"

King Jonah lowered the craft until it set down on the high grass. Jumping out, he ran over to the WomanForm, kneeling to place two fingers on her neck.

"She's alive!" he called to his soldiers. "Grab a gurney to put her on!"

He saw the skeleton lying next to her.

"Bring two gurneys and two blankets!" he ordered.

Looking up to inspect the old craft, he turned to the sergeant. "Alert the transportation staff to get a rescuer out here that's large enough to take this craft back to Maieman. It has a Platirian seal, but I'm not sending it to Platirius. I want to inspect it."

Peering at the skeleton again, he said, "I want a full scan done on these bones too." He nodded in the WomanForm's direction. "This is Queen Vivant's general. The closest medical chamber is JanIus. We'll take her there."

"Yes, My King!"

Surrounded by endless rows of indigo delphiniums as far as the eye could see, King Jonah shook his head in amazement.

"What in Maieman were you doing out here, General Lyric?"

*K*ing Asa awakened in one of Queen Vivant's majestic gardens. Concentrating on watering the large blue roses towering above her, she didn't notice when he approached her.

Five crowns were suspended above her head, rotating in a circle. As he moved closer, he saw five baby rabbits of various hues—red, purple, and three silver ones—running around her feet.

He started to call her name, then stepped back. At his feet sat a large, bright blue frog facing a slightly smaller green one.

The queen set the water can down and sat on the lush, platinum grass. The rabbits piled into her lap, lying still under her hands. Lovingly, she stroked their fur, humming a soft lullaby.

When a MaleForm, dressed in black, appeared and grabbed one of the silver rabbits, the water can was replaced by her BrainStaff. She jumped to her feet, grabbed it, and stabbed him in the heart.

The rabbit dropped from his hand, scurrying off to be with the others. He watched the blue frog eat the green frog, and the MaleForm disintegrated into dust. Strong billowing winds came to sweep him away.

King Asa slowly opened his eyes and sat up. A shadowy figure stood in the corner. He watched it step into the light and flung himself out of bed, falling at its feet.

"Greetings to you, King Asa of Onzi. I am Joshua, an angel in The One's army. I've been sent to inform you Queen Vivant, His Protector of Earth, is in grave danger."

The angel stood over the trembling king.

"Upon escaping from hell, King Anemi perverted Heaven's laws and stole the queen's vessel. His Majesty, The One, has assigned you to send him back. Do you accept the assignment?"

King Asa kept his face pressed to the floor. His quavering voice sounded unfamiliar. "Yes, I do."

"The One has spoken to you through a dream. Do you know what it means?"

He tried to remember what he'd witnessed. "I'm not sure what the frogs represent, but the rabbits...I think they were Vivant's family. She was protecting them against him."

The angel's countenance was illuminated in the dark bed chamber. "Is there more?"

"Seven," whispered the king. "Five rabbits, and two frogs. Seven. Seven symbolizes completion. The five crowns above her head are significant to getting Vivant back, too."

"Excellent," said the Angel Joshua. "Under Platirius, the four most powerful realms in the galaxy are Revani, Onzi, Maieman, and JanIus. The rabbits represent family. The frogs symbolize a former ruler conquering King Anemi. Please stand and listen to what you must do."

He was still shaking when the dining staff served breakfast.

Delila, one of his best dining staff, placed a bowl of porridge and a dish of ackee and saltfish before him. "My King, have you taken ill? You look as if you've seen a spirit!"

Strong-brewed coffee sloshed out of the cup when his trembling hands set it down. He licked the hot liquid off his hand.

"I'm fine, Delila. Thank you, I won't be needing anything else now."

He rubbed his weary eyes and sighed. He had no appetite, but forced himself to eat. Long days were ahead of him. He couldn't afford to make a mistake.

King Justin found Fawn struggling to get out of bed. A NurseForm stood on each side, trying to convince her to lie down.

"Dr. Azini, please let us help you. That's what we're here for!"

Fawn shook her head. "I can do it myself!"

"What's going on here?" he asked, racing toward her.

Catching her off guard, he moved a NurseForm aside and swung her legs up onto the bed.

"My King, she has a catheter, but she wants to use the bath chamber!"

"It's uncomfortable," muttered Fawn. "Now that I'm awake, there's no reason to wear it."

"Leave us, please," he ordered. "I'll call you when we're finished here."

The NurseForms bowed and exited the bed chamber.

"Now you listen to me, Dr. Azini. Less than seventy-two hours ago, you had brain surgery. Now you think you can get up and roam about? Nope! There's no way I'm letting that happen."

He covered her with a soft, warm blanket. "I know you're used to giving orders, but until you're well again, you'll follow *this* doctor's orders."

"But..." she protested.

"No buts," he murmured, easing her into the cozy, plush mattress. "Are you questioning your king?"

Biting down on her bottom lip, she said, "Of course not. Who performed the surgery?"

Smiling, he grabbed a high stool and positioned himself on it.

"I did!" he said proudly.

Her eyes grew larger than a craft. "You? But no ruler is permitted to have a dual role."

"Think about what you just said. Does that sound right to you?"

Reluctantly, she shook her head no.

"I don't know who invented that rule, but I tossed it the second you passed out in my arms. I won't fight you on letting me come back to work at the institute, but I'm going to take good care of you." His green eyes twinkled at her. "And I don't need anyone's permission to do it—not even yours, my gorgeous little doctor."

My gorgeous little doctor!

Since her father had worn down her self-esteem, she didn't consider herself to be attractive. She hoped the flames were tormenting him in hell. Still, her king's words warmed her heart. Shifting uncomfortably in the bed, she said, "This catheter is driving me crazy!"

He fluffed up a pillow and gently eased her head down on it.

"You're in no position to be on your feet right now. How about a bedpan? Would that help?"

She frowned. "I don't want to do that either. It's embarrassing."

"Then tell me what to do to make you comfortable." He ran a patch of her curls through his fingertips. "I'll do anything for you, Fawn."

Her heart fluttered. His rich, deep tone was as gentle as a caress.

Get yourself together, Fawn! This isn't a Human soap opera!

"I'll...I'll take the bedpan." Tugging on the catheter cord, she said, "I just want this removed!"

He snapped his fingers. "Done. Is anyone out there?" he called.

"Yes, Your Highness! We are!"

"Bring a bedpan in here, please? Dr. Azini wants the catheter removed."

"Yes, King Justin."

"I'll leave while they take it out."

She said it before she could stop herself. "Will you return?"

"Oh yes. I'll be right outside the door. We have a lot to catch up on."

She melted when he winked at her. "I'm not going anywhere."

Just as he positioned himself outside of her door, a code red sounded.

Captain Amara rushed through the door. "My King! King Jonah is bringing General Lyric to the institute! She's been hurt!"

"What? What happened?"

He saw King Jonah and Queen Marietta running beside a stretcher, headed toward the institute.

"We don't know yet, Your Highness!"

He took off with the captain following right behind him and ran inside just as the medical staff hurried her into a private chamber.

He nodded at them. "King Jonah. Queen Marietta. What happened to her?"

"I don't know. I found her out in the Averlands. My guess is she fell from one of the high cliffs. I didn't move her. If something is broken, I didn't want to make it worse."

"Where's her mother?" asked King Justin.

King Jonah looked dumbfounded. "Her mother? I thought she was dead?"

"She is," said Queen Marietta. "She was thrown into the Flames of Justice when Lyric was a ChildForm."

"Not anymore," said King Justin. "Someone released her."

Queen Marietta closed her eyes briefly, then opened them. "He won't stop until all of us are destroyed."

King Justin turned to her. "Who?"

"King Justin, there's something we need to discuss," said Queen Marietta. "It can't be put off any longer. Vivant is in danger, and it will take all of us joining together to save her."

"What's wrong with Aunt Vivant?"

"If you'll set up a time to meet, I'll tell you everything you need to know. We'll need your mother's assistance too."

"She and my Aunt Legend have returned to Revani. They were here to help take care of Colonel Azini. I expect them back by the week's end."

Queen Marietta shook her head. "That will be much too late. We need her now."

He surveyed the queen's worried expression. "This isn't going to be good, is it?"

"It's the worst thing that could've happened to all of us," she said.

He looked at King Jonah. "Did you find any clues out there? Anything to tell you how and why she was out there?"

"I found an old Platirian craft and a skeleton," said King Jonah. "My research staff is working on them now to find some answers. I need to get back to Maieman. I want to know the skeleton's identity."

Queen Marietta caught his arm. "Stay for a moment, Jonah. This is far more important. If we don't deal with this, more will die. If we're going to stand and fight, it has to be now!"

He swore. "You're right, Mother. Alright, I'll stay."

King Justin pressed a button on the NurseForm station. "Attention, everyone! General Barrios, Princess Teenah, Tarah, Tyre, Colonel Lionus, Captain Amara, Sergeant Caleb, and Sergeant Elisha, please report to my meeting chamber." He turned to Queen Marietta. "I should probably dispatch the Vivacians so you can fill them in too."

She shook her head. "No, not Vivant's army. Only Advisor TamRi."

"Why not?"

"Her warriors are much too close to Vivant. If he starts suspecting them, everything could blow up in our faces. Advisor TamRi is one of The One's soldiers. I suspect he's been avoiding her because he can't hide from her, nor can he control her."

King Justin shook his head in frustration. "I still don't know who this 'he' is, but I'll have her dispatched here immediately."

"Thank you, King Justin."

"You're welcome. Go ahead. I'll meet up with you as soon as I find out what's going on with General Lyric."

"I love what's happening between Justin and Fawn," gushed General Legend. "New love is so intoxicating!"

Queen Revari poured a steaming cup of lemon and ginger tea. "Mmm. She'll be much better for him than Lyric. Tea?"

General Legend looked at the small bags of herbs. "Peppermint for me, please? I would say I'm surprised Lady Alarah ended her, but I'm not. As for Lady Alarah, she should've been put down a long time ago."

The queen poured hot water over the tea bags, added sugar, and then cream before handing the cup to the general.

"I never wanted to see Lyric dead, but Lady Alarah served her purpose. Now she's on the run. No one in the galaxy will take her in. They know better than to cross me."

"King Jonah put out an APB too. Can you believe it?"

Queen Revari sipped her tea. "I can. He's been pining after my sister ever since he discovered what the tool between his legs is supposed to do!"

She and General Legend cackled.

"REVARI!"

General Legend got up to look out of the window. "Who on Revani is that?" She gasped. "By The One! It can't be!"

"REVARI!"

"Who is it, Legend?"

Queen Revari got up and stood next to her. Together, they spied the tall figure marching across the expansive gold lawn.

His eyes locked with hers.

Colonel Sheila burst into the chamber. "My Queen! It's—"

"General Kron," said Queen Revari. "Have you come to die again?" she called down to him. Grabbing her BrainStaff, she said, "Alright. Back to Hell's streets you go!"

"Her back is broken, Your Highness," said Dr. Clint. "She won't be going anywhere anytime soon." He shook his head. "She's lucky to be alive."

King Justin grabbed her hand. "King Jonah said she's been unconscious since he found her. I don't believe Lyric was on that mountain alone. Someone got her up there and left her there to die. If it's who I think it is, her days are numbered."

Her face and arms were covered with scratches and bruises.

"You're going to be okay, Lyric."

Her eyes flew open. "Justin?"

He leaned into her. "Lyric! Thank The One you're awake! Don't try to move. Dr. Clint says your back is broken. Do you remember what happened? Why were you in the Averlands?"

She grimaced. Pain shot through her body like lightning. "My—it was my mother. My mother pushed me off the cliff. She said…"

She bit her lip, trying to hold back tears. "She said my father was alive, so I went with her. But it was a lie. There's a body there, but I don't think it belongs to my father. She said awful things to me."

He wiped the tears spilling down her face. "Justin, months ago, she told me you had a new TeleScreen number. Every time I called, your assistant said you were busy. And every time I planned a date, you'd cancel at the last minute."

He blinked as if she'd slapped him. "Wait a minute. I don't have an assistant, and I've never made or cancelled any dates with you. The last time I saw you was when we had supper at your cottage!"

Her heart sank. "That was last fall! Then she's been lying to me all this time. She burned everything you bought me, including the roses. My clothes, the jewelry—I found it all burned in the fireplace!" She burst into a fresh round of tears. "She never loved me, Justin! She never loved me!"

His heart shattered. Dr. Clint stopped him from taking her into his arms. "We don't want to move her, My King." He paused. "I haven't ruled out partial paralysis yet."

Taking out a sharp instrument, he stuck it into one of her thighs. "General, can you feel this?"

She blinked. "No."

Moving it to the other leg, he asked, "How about now?"

Anxiety rose in her. "No! I can't feel anything. Oh! I can't feel my legs!" she shouted.

"It's okay, Lyric," said King Justin. "Listen to me! You just woke up. Your body hasn't had time to recover from the fall. I know it's hard, but please don't panic. You're in good hands. This will pass, I promise you!"

Sticking his head outside of the door, he said, "I want an all-points bulletin filed on Lady Alarah Iham. Get her picture posted on every TeleScreen and TranScreen! Find her and drag her to me!"

Captain Amara saluted him! "Yes, My King!"

He grabbed the general's hand again. "You're one of the strongest WomenForms I know. I need you to fight like you've never fought before, do you hear me?"

She looked up at him, chilled by the anger burning in his eyes. She hadn't noticed how much he resembled Queen Revari when he was furious.

"She won't get away with this. I promise you that." He pulled the blanket up to her chin. "Dr. Clint, I have to get back. Please take care of her and send reports to me every hour!"

"You got it, My King!" said Dr. Clint. "We'll take good care of you, General Lyric. I'm the best in my field, you know."

General Lyric tried to let his words comfort her, but she couldn't. If she couldn't walk, she'd never be a general again. She couldn't live without her career. She noticed for all of his kind words, Justin didn't seem as affectionate as he once was.

She tried convincing herself maybe he didn't want to show emotion in front of Dr. Clint, but she knew him better than that. He'd never cared about such things before. In a single act of cruelty, her mother might've destroyed her career and her relationship. She allowed her tears to fall hard and fast, not feeling them when they landed on her neck.

D omi stood before King Asa.

"Your sister has been in an accident. According to the APBs, the culprit is your mother. She pushed General Lyric off a cliff!"

"By The One! Is Lyric still alive, My King?"

"Yes, she's awake, but it doesn't look good. King Justin says she may be paralyzed. He's requested that you see her."

He pulled up battle sleeves over his arms. "I'm going with you. I have business to discuss with him."

"Lyric invited me to have dinner with them last fall. I sensed she was evil then. She pretended to be nice in front of Lyric, but after she went to the bath chamber, I saw who she really was. She told me I was a disgrace and I'd never hold a candle to Lyric. I got so angry, I left without saying goodbye. I never told Lyric what happened."

She broke down in tears. "Maybe if I had, she wouldn't have gotten the chance to hurt her. Lyric might've listened to me and kept an eye on her. But it's too late!"

Taking a linen napkin out of his shirt, he handed it to her. "It does no good to blame yourself now. One Being did this—Lady Alarah. Come, let us get to JanIus!"

King Justin hurried back to Fawn.

"I'm so sorry! I had an emergency to take care of!"

"What's happened?" asked Fawn frantically. "Who was taken to the institute?"

He raised his hands in the air. "The only thing I want you concentrating on is your recovery. We have highly trained medical staff, and thanks to you, they run a tight ship. Please trust them to handle things."

Fawn lowered herself onto the pillows, waving her hand to raise the head of the bed.

Taking both of her hands in his, he said, "I have everything under control, Fawn. Do you trust me?"

"Of course I do. I know how competent you are."

Giving them a gentle squeeze, he said, "Good. You don't know how much that means to me."

A NurseForm entered. "Dr. Azini? I brought your lunch! Chicken broth and pureed fruit!"

King Justin laughed when Fawn groaned. "You need to work your way up to solid food. I promise this tastes a lot better than the hospital food I've tried during my residency."

Taking the spoon from Fawn, he guided a bit of broth to her lips.

"Mmmm. It *is* good!" she said.

"See? I told you! Now eat up. I'll be back when...I have everything handled."

Fawn sensed something was wrong. "And I won't be there to help you! I hate that!"

His eyes reminded her of sparkling emeralds. "You're helping me now. Seeing you smile and talk with me is air in my lungs."

She hoped he didn't notice her blushing. "Is there anything I can do?"

"Yes," he said, kissing her cheek. "Get better fast!"

The NurseForm's eyes got wide, then shifted to an imaginary cobweb in a corner when King Justin's gaze slid to her.

"Take good care of my colonel!" he said. "I'll be back!"

"Yes, Your Highness!"

Advisor TamRi sat at the large conference table with King Justin, his trusted soldiers, and the heads of Maieman.

"I understand why you wanted me here, but how is it fair to Colonel Kourtney, Major Sonee, and Sergeants Alicia and Thea to be kept in the dark? They're in danger every second they're with King Anemi!"

"If he knows the Vivacians are on to him, he won't hesitate to kill them," said Queen Marietta. "It must be driving him crazy to have an all WomanForm army. If he attacks one of our realms, we have to fight against them without hurting them."

"That's easier said than done, Queen Marietta," said Gallium. "How did he get to Queen Vivant anyway?"

"He must've caught her at a weak moment. It happens to all of us. The Enemy attacks when we're most vulnerable."

"How do we get him to release her?" asked King Jonah.

"We can't. He couldn't have taken over Vivant unless her defenses were down. She has to be the one to break his hold. Once they're separated, that's where you and Gallium come in, Advisor TamRi. If you touch him, he'll become flesh again. He can't win against two supernatural Beings. With the two of you working together, it'll be easier to kill him and send him back to Hell."

"But what will make her want to separate from him?" asked King Justin. "If she stood by and watched him try to marry off her daughters, then doesn't that mean she's complicit?"

"No," said King Asa, entering the chamber. "It doesn't. Vivant doesn't know what he's doing. She's in a world she's created in her mind to deal with her pain. He overpowered her when she traveled back to it after King Belial was defeated. I don't believe she allowed him to take over her vessel. As Queen Marietta said, he caught her at a weak moment."

"How do we get her to return?" asked Princess Tyre.

"You," said King Asa. "Her family is at the center of her pain. She'd do anything for you—even give her life. An arranged marriage may be an inconvenience, but it's not dangerous. Queen Vivant has to see one or more of you is in danger. Then she'll break free."

"But—"

Gallium's TeleScreen beeped. It was General Legend.

"Gallium! Revani is under attack! It's—"

"BARRIOS!!!" someone thundered.

Gallium, Queen Marietta, and King Jonah stood.

"It can't be!" cried Queen Marietta.

"COME TO ME, GALLIUM BARRIOS!"

In a rage, Gallium started shaking. Colonel Lionus gawked at the TeleScreen. The tall figure flung Queen Revari off his back and connected a solid punch to General Legend's jaw.

Gallium's power exploded, blowing everyone out of their seats. "KRON!!!" he shouted.

Colonel Lionus jumped on his back as he shot up and out of the chamber, hurling furiously toward Revani.

The princesses looked at each other in shock. "That was our father!" cried Princess Tarah.

"Let us go!" shouted Queen Marietta. "We have to get to Revani!"

"We're coming too!" cried Princess Tyre.

"No!" said Queen Marietta. "He's not himself! I don't want you to get hurt."

"Grandmother, Aunt Revari trained us how to fight!"

"Yes, but who will you fight?" asked King Asa. "He doesn't know who you are anymore. If he turns on you, are you ready to end your own father?"

"We're going!" said Princess Tarah firmly. "Grandmother, please take us to him!"

King Jonah raced to his craft. A nagging suspicion pricked his conscience, but he had to know if his brother was really alive.

I'm coming, Lucian. I'm coming!

D omi set the bouquet of pink roses on the bedside table.

"I don't think pink is your color, but I was in a hurry. How are you feeling?"

General Lyric didn't take her eyes off the rain beating against the windows. "Worthless."

"Oh, Lyric. None of this was your fault."

"How could I not see her for what she was? Justin despised her on sight." She winced. "She played games right in my face, but I couldn't see it. No, that's not true."

She turned to face Domi. "There were times when I felt something was wrong. Sometimes things didn't make sense, but I wouldn't let myself see the truth. Every time I got a sick feeling, I ignored it."

Domi sat by her bed. "I should've told you how mean she was to me the night I came to dinner. Maybe if I had, you wouldn't be here right now."

General Lyric turned to her. "That was one of the things I ignored—you disappearing on me. I told myself you weren't ready to embrace her like I was. Now here I am. No good to anyone."

Domi started to say something when a loud blast echoed through the chamber. She held on to General Lyric when the ground shook.

"My King!" she called to King Asa on her TeleScreen.

"**G**eneral Kron is alive!" said King Asa. "Who would've thought it?"

"And he's attacking my mother," said King Justin. "I have to get over there too!"

Just as he grabbed his BrainStaff, a loud explosion rang through JanIus and knocked them off their feet.

"What the hell was that?" shouted King Justin.

He, King Asa, Advisor TamRi, and the JanIan soldiers ran into the center of the courtyard. Wreckage was everywhere. Deja vu swept over King Justin as he looked around at the debris, fallen trees, and a large, gaping hole in the palace's roof.

Above them stood King Anemi and the Vivacians.

Domi's frantic voice sounded through King Asa's TeleScreen. "My King!"

"Stand down, Domi. All Onzian soldiers, stand down! We're not attacking the Platirians."

King Justin whirled to stare at him.

King Asa met his steely gaze without flinching. "Queen Marietta and I laid out everything for you. You'll have to find a way to defend yourselves without hurting Queen Vivant. If you do, I'll kill you."

"What the hell are you saying?" demanded King Justin. "You're just going to leave us hanging?"

"I'd say General Kron was a ruse to get rid of half of your help and a damned good one. For now, you're on your own." Thrusting his chin toward the sky, he said, "You have bigger things to worry about than me, King Justin."

King Anemi pointed Queen Vivant's BrainStaff at him. "I'll ask you once, King Justin, where are my daughters?"

Chapter 8

When General Kron saw Gallium speeding toward him, he flung Colonel Angela off him like a wet dishrag and ran in the direction of the light. Their collision made a loud explosion that threw everyone to the ground. Queen Marietta sat behind the controls, following closely behind in her craft.

I need to see his face. I need to know if it's really him!

King Jonah turned his craft to align with hers just in time to see General Kron fighting with Gallium, Colonel Lionus, and the JanIan soldiers that had followed to take him down. The general turned to look up at the incoming crafts.

His empty eyes showed no sign of recognition for the king and queen.

"He looks...strange," said Princess Teenah.

"Lucian?" asked Queen Marietta. "Lucian, it's Mother!"

The general detonated a bomb, sending everyone, except Gallium, running. It exploded, creating a cloud of smoke.

Queen Marietta pulled on the controls, attempting to get around it, when she felt a heavy weight drop on top of the craft. When the smoke cleared, she and General Kron were face to face.

His empty stare chilled her to her core. He reached back and punched violently at the craft's shield, blood splattering from his hand as he tried to break through it.

"Mother!" shouted King Jonah.

General Kron whipped his head around at him and fired into his craft. King Jonah ducked, circling the craft around the queen's. The general fired again, this time at the engine. The craft rocked violently back and forth when the shot hit home.

"Jonah!" screamed Queen Marietta.

The general turned back to her, his soulless eyes balefully staring at her.

"Father! It's us!" cried Princess Tarah.

She shuddered when he looked through her. An ugly, jagged scar traveled from the top of his head and down his cheek. Growling menacingly, he punched at the window again.

"What's wrong with him?" asked Princess Tyre. "Why does he look like that?"

The WomenForms screamed when Gallium flung him off the craft. Together, they hurled toward the ground. Gallium fell on top of him, planting hard blows to his damaged face.

The general stuck a long dagger in Gallium's neck and kicked him off of him, just in time to grab Queen Revari by the neck, slamming her to the ground. Sergeant Kiana felt a vicious kick to the face before she went down. He stomped on her head several times before reaching down to slit her throat.

Colonel Sheila jumped on his back, stabbing him in the back of the neck with a blade. When he grabbed her arm and bit it, she sank her teeth into his face. Queen Revari drove her BrainStaff deep into his gut, while General Legend stabbed him in the side.

He threw all of the female soldiers as if they weighed no more than flies. Queen Marietta parked the craft.

Grabbing King Micah's BrainStaff, she said, "Come on, soldiers! We can't let him kill Queen Revari!"

King Jonah and the Maieman soldiers were right behind her and the princesses.

"Lucian! It's Jonah! Please stop! Look, here are your daughters and our mother. We're your family!"

General Kron turned and looked at him. "I have no family!"

King Justin stared up at King Anemi. "I don't want to hurt you, Aunt Vivant! Please don't do this!"

"You can call him by his name now," said Advisor TamRi. "Look at the eyes of the Vivacians. They're all under his spell."

She was right. The eyes of Queen Vivant's soldiers were just as black as King Anemi's.

"Let her go, Grandfather!" bellowed King Justin.

King Anemi laughed while pinching his thumb and forefinger together. "Let her go? Now why would I do that when I'm this close to ruling Platirius again? But if you really want to see her gone, you can set her free." He pointed at King Justin's BrainStaff. "End her and it'll all be over."

Advisor TamRi's voice entered his mind.

He wants you to kill Queen Vivant. He thinks his spirit will enter another host, but it isn't true. The queen is one of The One's servants. As punishment for corrupting her, they both will die, but he doesn't know that.

How do I reach her? Can you see her?

I can. She's in a garden! A powerful presence is with her. It's protecting her! She won't leave the space she's created.

King Justin swore.

King Anemi smiled craftily. "I can make you end her, King Justin."

When he waved his hand, a scene shimmered in the sky. Oliver Ascencio, suspended by his feet, hung in the air. A group of soldiers stood around him. One soldier hit him with a blast of electricity. His tormentors laughed when he vomited.

"What's the matter, Human? You feel sick? Here. Let me wipe your mouth!"

He wrapped a piece of plastic around Oliver's face, smothering him. With his hands bound behind his back, he struggled to get air into his lungs.

"By The One!" said King Asa.

"Stop it, you demon!" shouted Advisor TamRi.

The soldier removed the plastic and tried to suffocate him again. "Damn! He's a hard one to kill, isn't he?"

"Please!" said Oliver. "Please, don't hurt Revari! Please?"

He screamed when another soldier doused his hair with fluid and set it on fire.

"The king is taking care of the princess. If I were you, I'd worry about myself!"

As a series of heinous acts followed, Advisor TamRi noted the rage building inside King Justin.

"It wasn't for Vivant, your father wouldn't have been tortured to death!" said King Anemi. "It's all her fault! End her! Take vengeance for your father."

King Anemi saw King Justin's grip tighten around his BrainStaff. "Go on. Show everyone here how a true king responds to his enemies."

King Asa's hand went to his BrainStaff, ready to fire on King Justin.

King Anemi looked at Captain Kourtney over his shoulder. "Kill the JanIans," he commanded.

With a loud war cry, the captain and the Vivacians launched into battle against the JanIan soldiers.

"*You vile monster!*" spat Advisor TamRi. Closing her eyes, she used her powers to make the dreadful scenes disappear. "Please, King Justin," she pleaded. "Don't hurt Queen Vivant!"

Controlled by a dark force, King Justin raised his BrainStaff.

R evaltian, JanIan, and Maieman soldiers encircled General Kron.

"We have to end this now," said Princess Teenah.

Unsheathing her sword, she moved closer to him.

"Teenah," cried Queen Marietta. "Come back!"

"Let her go, Grandmother. She knows what she's doing," said Princess Tyre.

"Who are you?" asked Princess Teenah.

"I am General Kron. General of Platirius," he said.

"What was your last mission?" she asked.

His head jerked strangely.

"Were you really dispatched to a battle outside of Platirius?"

Silence. When he began closing the distance between them, Gallium got ready to pounce.

"Halt, Gallium," commanded Princess Teenah. "I've got this."

When he was close enough to touch, she said, "Where's my candy?"

General Kron stopped abruptly, his vacant stare as empty as a forgotten dimension in Space.

The princess raised her sword. "You're not my father!"

She swung and cut his head off. Swiftly, his hands reached for her, but Queen Revari and Gallium cut him down. They sliced off both of his legs, leaving him to collapse in the dirt. He jerked and twitched until he fell still.

"It's a clone!" said Princess Teenah. "Just a stupid clone!"

A dispatch from Maieman sounded through King Jonah's TeleScreen. "King Jonah? It's Sergeant Reed!"

"Go ahead, Sergeant Reed!" said King Jonah.

"The body you brought here. We know who it is. The results are 100% positive!"

King Jonah's breath caught. Princess Tarah ran to steady him when his knees buckled. "It's my brother, isn't it?"

"Yes, My King. It's General Lucian Kron!"

King Jonah fell to his knees and wept. Queen Marietta and the princesses kneeled and wrapped their arms around him. He wailed loudly, rocking back and forth on his haunches.

Queen Revari turned to Gallium. "This was probably a ruse to get you away from JanIus! But why?"

King Jonah sobbed. "I felt it. But I didn't want to believe it. You knew, didn't you, Mama?"

She nodded, holding him tightly. "Yes. I knew it the moment he tried to attack me through the glass. Lucian's mind was too strong. No magic could make him raise a hand to me."

Queen Revari quickly inspected her Revaltians. "Anyone who's been badly injured, report to the medical chamber. The rest of you, come with me! We have to get to JanIus!"

"It's okay to go back to Maieman to be with Father, Grandmother," said Princess Teenah. "We'll go back and help Mother."

"No," said Queen Marietta. "I've lost one of my sons. I won't lose my daughter too. Stand, King Jonah. You have to stand now. For Vivant."

He wiped his face. "Let us go, troops! To JanIus!"

Gallium hugged General Legend. "Are you alright?"

"Of course," she said. "Come on! King Justin needs us!"

The reinforcements arrived just as King Justin raised his BrainStaff to fire on Queen Vivant.

Queen Marietta ran from her craft and stood in front of him. She glared up at King Anemi.

"It's all over! We discovered your dirty little secret! You tried to turn that *thing* into my son, but it didn't work! I know you know what happened to him! Tell me what happened to Lucian!"

Seeing King Anemi's cruel smile on Queen Vivant's face cut through her soul.

"Alright, Queen Marietta. Since you asked so politely."

He waved his hand, and an image appeared of General Kron crawling on the ground. Working the parachute off his legs with his feet, he tried to sit up and fell back, panting harshly. King Anemi materialized out of thin air, looking down at him.

"It looks as if you've lost your way, soldier."

He rolled the general over with his foot and kneeled at his side.

"Platirius has yet to lose a war. I blame you for that. As long as my son has you, he'll be victorious in every battle. I didn't build it for his legacy—it's for my own!"

Covering General Kron's nose and mouth, he pressed down hard. The general tried desperately to move his hand, but the poison he'd consumed was coursing through his veins, weakening him.

"It's funny," said King Anemi. "Had Marietta married me instead of your foolish father, you would've been my son. I'd be alive now, planning your coronation to succeed me on the throne."

Increasing the pressure, he said, "The only thing my granddaughter will plan now is your DeathCeremony."

The general's legs shuffled furiously in the grass, kicking up dirt. He struggled against King Anemi's iron grip with all his might. As darkness crept over him, lulling him into submission, his chest rose for a final time, then collapsed. King Anemi released him, allowing his head to fall to the ground.

"Your father should've never allowed you to come to Platirius. He signed your death warrant."

General Kron's sightless eyes stared up into Space. The king rose and looked around.

"No one has used this land for years. There's no chance you'll be found until it's too late—maybe never. It's the price your mother paid for crossing me." He kicked at the general's face. "Farewell, General Kron. One more thorn in my side has been plucked."

His cruel laughter faded as he disappeared, leaving General Kron's body to cool in the desolate tundra.

King Jonah glared at him while Queen Marietta and the princesses wept.

"You bastard," she said. "You killed my baby in the midst of him fighting to come home to us!"

He pointed at her before jerking his thumb at himself. "You never should've let him leave, Marietta! This is on you and Micah, not me! But you can always take your vengeance." He raised his arms in the air. "Come on. Kill this vessel. Get justice for your son!"

"You really take me for a fool? I'll never give you the chance to return to Platirius!"

"Look at all the enemies standing around. Vivant's Vivacians. Revari and her Revaltians. King Justin and his JanIans. King Asa and his Onzians!"

Glaring at Advisor TamRi and Gallium, he said, "And who could forget The One's special pets! My grandson is still foaming at the mouth after watching his father die like the animal he was. I can *feel* how much he wants Vivant dead!"

"What's he talking about?" Queen Revari asked Advisor TamRi. "What has he done to Justin?"

Advisor TamRi kept her eyes on King Anemi. "You don't want to know how he's been playing with King Justin's head, Queen Revari."

Queen Marietta glanced at King Justin out of the corner of her eye. His gaze was fixated on King Anemi. She couldn't tell if what he said was true or not.

"Vivant won't return on her own," said King Anemi. "She knows she's done too much to come back and reign. No one trusts her now."

"Lies!" cried Queen Marietta. "My daughter has done nothing wrong! All of this madness will be laid at your feet, Anemi!"

He waved her off. "She's content to let me rule Platirius, and I shall. You can't stop me. No one can!"

"Aunt Vivant, I know you're in there," said King Justin. "I don't want to hurt you, but I won't allow Anemi to take over again."

Pointing his BrainStaff at King Anemi, he said, "It's not about what happened to my father—it's about right and wrong. Anemi has done his homework, but he didn't study the CliffNotes. If he dies in the stolen vessel of The One's servant, he dies for all of eternity."

King Anemi's eye twitched. For the first time since attacking JanIus, he looked unsure of himself.

"Please. Show us a sign you're in there."

"Please don't kill our mother!" cried Princess Teenah.

King Justin's eyes filled with tears. "I don't have a choice."

Queen Revari moved closer to him. "Justin, you can't," she cried.

"We can't let him win!" said King Justin.

"If you touch her, I'll destroy you," promised King Asa.

Everyone turned to look at King Asa.

"If I don't, King Anemi will take over everything!" shouted King Justin.

"If you harm Vivant, I'll turn your everything into nothing!" countered King Asa. "As far as I'm concerned, except for her daughters, she can kill everyone here."

Queen Revari glared at him. "Did you just threaten my son?"

King Asa took a step toward her. "I threatened him *and* you!"

"This isn't helping!" said Advisor TamRi. "We have to work together to defeat him!"

"The thought of a WomanForm leading a revolution against me makes me sick," muttered King Anemi.

He aimed the BrainStaff at Queen Marietta and fired.

"Noooo!" said Princess Teenah, bolting in front of the queen. A collective shout soared through the courtyard when the blast ripped through her.

"TEENAH!" screamed Queen Marietta, reaching out to break her fall.

A loud cry sounded in the air. The Vivacians stopped fighting with the JanIans. All eyes were on Platirius's leader. King Asa motioned the Onzians back as another cry rang out. Queen Vivant's body began to shake just as Advisor TamRi reached it and separated King Anemi's spirit from her queen's.

Raising one hand toward The One's realm, she covered his mouth with her other hand, muting his powers and making him flesh and blood.

An enraged Queen Vivant began dismembering him with her BrainStaff. She severed his arms and legs before lopping off his head. Blood trickled down from the sky as she delivered vicious blows. She continued stabbing and cutting, his blood splattering on her face and hair.

Once everyone realized she wasn't going to stop, Gallium and General Legend flung themselves on her. With strength he hadn't known she possessed, she grabbed him by the neck and threw him into Space.

General Legend screamed when the queen's fist punched a hole through the muscle and tissue of her thigh. Gallium rushed to hold her, while Advisor TamRi used her powers to restore the damage that had been done to her leg.

Years of suppressed rage that had been building inside her since she lost her mother were finally unleashed. King Anemi's body, now a bloody pulp of mangled tissue and bones, remained the object of her fury.

King Asa remembered the frogs in his dream. He kneeled next to Gallium, whispering in his ear. When Gallium gaped at him, he said, "Open the gateway. It's the only way to stop her."

Gallium handed General Legend to Queen Revari and joined hands with Advisor TamRi. Thunder and lightning ripped through the air. Everyone stepped back when The One's realm opened, revealing a shadow walking through it.

"VIVANT ELIZABETH AMOROUS! STAND DOWN!"

Princess Teenah sat up in Queen Marietta's arms.

"I'm alright, Grandmother! I activated my protective shield before the blast caught me."

Queen Marietta caressed her face. The princesses joined their grandmother in embracing their sister.

"Look," whispered Princess Tarah. "Just look at her!"

Everyone turned to see Queen Dellah standing among the clouds.

"It's over now, daughter. You've defeated him. Let it go, Vivant!"

The Surveyors' voices shimmered across the sky. *"Queen Dellah's planet was Coldarius, a deep, vibrant blue. Blue is the universal hue of peace."*

Queen Vivant dropped her BrainStaff, falling to her knees, sobbing openly. All knees—royalty and soldiers—bowed to the former Queen of Platirius. Just as it had happened in King Asa's dream, a blue mist engulfed what was left of King Anemi before a thick cloud of black dust rose into the air and disappeared. The princesses ran to their blood-soaked mother, holding her in their arms.

"I'm alright, Mother! It's okay," said Princess Teenah, kissing her. "Great-Grandfather has gone back to Hell where he belongs!"

"I'm sorry!" wailed Queen Vivant. "I'm so sorry!"

Queen Marietta ran to her, embracing her. "There's nothing to be sorry for! You didn't do anything wrong!"

The WomenForms moved back when Queen Dellah's spirit appeared in front of Queen Vivant. She lifted Queen Vivant's head in her hands.

"Everyone falls. No Being has the power to stand tall in the face of adversity all the time, Vivant. Anemi struck when you were most vulnerable, when you thought you'd lost me, but you didn't." She placed a finger over her daughter's heart, then the side of her head. "I am here and here. And I always will be."

Queen Dellah slightly pivoted her head. "Come to me, my little one!"

Queen Revari moved like lightning toward her. In awe, she kneeled before their beautiful mother. Queen Dellah lifted her to her feet, caressing her face in her hands.

"Both of you have endured so much pain for so many years. It's time to break free of it and love each other again."

Queen Revari cried as Queen Dellah restored all of her memories of when she and her sister were younger. She saw Queen Vivant feeding her and taking her out to play in King Carlomon's gardens.

Tears rolled down her face as memories of all the loving times she and her sister shared were renewed. She sobbed uncontrollably at a memory of Queen Vivant trying to comfort her cries at their mother's DeathCeremony.

Queen Dellah wrapped her arms around her. "I've tried to come to you through your dreams as I did with Vivant. But you wouldn't allow me to."

"I shut you out," whispered Queen Revari. "I was so angry with you for leaving me. And angry with myself for killing you!"

"You didn't kill me, Revari. It was my time to go. Now it's time for you and Vivant to let go of all the guilt and rage you've been holding inside. It's done nothing but keep our family apart. Please let it go. For me."

"Yes...M–M–Mama," blubbered Queen Revari.

Queen Dellah turned to the princesses and Queen Marietta. "Thank you for taking care of my family for me."

"They're my family too. You would've done the same for me."
She reached for Queen Dellah's hand. "I've missed you, old
friend."

Queen Dellah embraced her. "I've missed you too, Marietta."

"And you," said Queen Dellah to the princesses. "What
shining examples you are."

Unaware the two queens had been friends, they stared at them
in awe. The trio cried when Queen Dellah took them into her
arms.

Inclining her head toward King Justin, she said, "Hail to you,
King of JanIus."

He couldn't hold back his tears any longer. Kneeling on both
knees, he pressed his face into the ground at her feet. She lifted
him and smiled.

"Rise, grandson. I'm not higher than The One."

He broke down when he felt her arms go around his waist.
Everyone was crying, except King Asa, who kneeled to Queen
Vivant and gathered her close to his heart.

Gallium and General Legend bowed before their former
queen, who planted kisses on their foreheads. "My two favorite
Coldarians. I am so proud of you," she said.

She turned to address everyone. "Today, you've defeated one
of the greatest and most evil forces ever to roam Platirius's
halls. Let it be written in your Halls of Records, the kingdoms
of JanIus, Maieman, and Onzi united with the queendoms of
Platirius and Revani to save my daughter, Queen Vivant, and
your galaxy. This day shall never be forgotten. Your bravery will

always be remembered in The One's realm. On this day, I bow to you. In a while, Keepers of the Realms."

King Justin embraced Queen Revari just as she reached for her mother, but her spirit had disappeared.

"Mother," she wailed. He held her in his arms, allowing her to cry.

Spying King Asa with Queen Vivant, she quickly dried her eyes. "Get off my sister," she snapped.

"Well, that didn't last long, did it?" quipped King Asa.

Shooting an irritated glance her way, he eased away from Queen Vivant. Queen Revari wrapped her arms around her, smiling when she fiercely returned her embrace. It was her turn to rock her older sister like a baby in the fading sunlight.

General Kron's DeathCeremony was held on a bright, sunny day. His daughters, dressed in Platirian military gear and their father's medals, saluted his DeathCraft as it was carried around his family's palace.

Queen Marietta, King Jonah, and Queen Vivant, seated on white and black horses, followed the general's DeathCraft for seven laps around the palace. He was laid to rest beside his father.

As he'd done for Dr. Krause many years ago, Queen Vivant threw several white roses into his grave. She kneeled in front of it, whispering softly to him.

"That wasn't you that haunted my dreams when I was addicted to Callidut. It was my conscience. I realize that now. When King Anemi had me trapped, I saw how hard you tried to return to me."

She sniffed and blew her nose on a napkin. "I want you to be free now, Lucian. I don't hate you for keeping my father's secret about Coldarius. You were a victim of his insanity too. I loved you then, and I love you now. I'll always love you. Please rest with King Micah. The worst is over, my love."

The princesses came to stand with her.

"In a while, Father," they said. "We love you."

Fawn knocked on General Lyric's door. "Hello, General, may I come in?"

General Lyric looked up and smiled. "Of course! How are you feeling, Dr. Azini?"

"I feel good! But let's talk about you. I came to see how you were doing."

The general did a little dance. "I'm back to my old self!"

Fawn laughed and clapped her hands. "That's wonderful news! I knew nothing could keep you down for long." Her tone turned serious. "Have they found your mother yet?"

General Lyric tapped her Azgoate. "No. But I can't wait. I'm getting released today. As soon as Queen Vivant returns from Maieman, I'll ask her if I can head up a search party. I want her brought to justice so badly, I can taste it!"

"I understand, believe me," said Fawn. "She shouldn't get away with what she did to you."

The general flashed one of her rare smiles. "Thank you. That means so much to me!"

"It's my pleasure. Well, I have your release papers here. All you have to do is sign them!"

She held out her palm to transmit them to her.

"Ah! It feels so good to finally be going home! Sergeant Thea told me my cottage has been under constant surveillance. I don't think she's crazy enough to go back there."

"I don't think so either," said Fawn. "Don't worry about it too much. Just concentrate on getting your life back."

General Lyric glanced at a group of bees pollinating cucumber flowers, then back at Fawn. "It'll be a life without Justin. He's changed. The vibe we had has shifted. I wouldn't be surprised if someone else has captured his heart. It's my fault, you know?"

Fawn sat on the bed beside her. "Give yourself some grace. So much has happened. You two have time to find your way back to each other."

"I wish I shared your optimism, Fawn, but I think he's checked out for good. You know me. I don't stick around where I'm not wanted."

"Have faith," said Fawn.

General Lyric hugged her. "Thank you so much for being you."

Fawn returned her embrace. "I don't know who else to be!"

They laughed together before Fawn got up to leave and saluted her.

"In a while, General!"

She made her way down the stairs to a small research chamber connected to the main medical chamber. A Being rested on a cool, chrome table. Uncovering its face, she peered down into it.

"Well now, you won't be terrorizing anyone else, will you?" she asked.

Sliding her palm over the Being's palm, she transmitted all of their funds into her personal account.

"How nice of you to pay me for all the pain and misery you've caused me." Domi smiled down at Lady Alarah's panicked expression. "Oh, don't look at me like that! Where you're going, you won't need funds."

She turned on the incinerator and pushed the table closer to it. Lady Alarah, realizing what she was about to do, tried to scream, but no sound came.

"You were right, Mother. Lyric and I are very different. No one knows this, but I'm a better murderer than my brother was. Unlike him, my method is much smoother. I never leave traces behind."

Pausing to look into her terrified eyes, she said, "Hurting Lyric was a mistake. I would've left you alone had you not done that. But you couldn't help yourself." She traced a heart on Lady Alarah's cheek. "Now it's time to pay the piper."

Tilting the table, she slid her mother into the incinerator and closed it. Holding her face to the door, she smiled until she couldn't hear her muffled screams anymore.

"It's not the Flames of Justice, but it'll do." Her smile faded. "Goodbye, Mother. I'll see you in Hell someday."

Epilogue

King Asa thrust wildly for the final time, causing another orgasm to quake Queen Vivant's body just as he emptied himself inside of her. Exhaling loudly, he rolled over until she lay on top of his chest. They lay together for a long while until their breathing slowed to a normal pace.

Tracing his pectoral with the tip of her manicured nail, she said, "I feel as if I've awakened from a long nightmare."

Stroking her back with his fingertips, he said, "I'm glad. I don't know what I would've done if I had lost you."

She looked up at him. "Do you mean that?"

"Of course I do." He rearranged the bed covers around them. "Listen, I know neither of us planned on love, but I've fallen for you. Hard. I've never been in love before, but somehow, you got inside my head."

She wrinkled her nose. "Like how King Anemi got inside of me?"

He groaned. "Don't even joke about that!"

She laughed aloud.

He kissed both dimples on her cheeks and the pear-shaped mole on her breast. "It's so good to hear you laughing again."

Pulling her closer to his muscular physique, he planted a kiss on her forehead. "How did it feel to finally let go of everything?"

She shuddered. "Terrifying. I even scared myself. I never realized how much pain I've been holding in for all these years." She nibbled on his bottom lip. "Where do we go from here?"

He gently caressed her bottom. "Anywhere you want. You need to understand something, Vivant. I don't love easily, but when I do, I love hard. I'm not going anywhere. I'll be around whenever you need me."

She touched his full lips with her fingertips. "You know, I think you're the only MaleForm in the whole galaxy who isn't afraid of my sister!"

He threw back his head and laughed. "I'm not the only one, but she isn't afraid of me either!"

Queen Vivant burst into laughter. "I can't remember when I've been this happy. I finally have my sister back, and my daughters...and now...you."

"You'll always have me, My Queen."

She noted the sincerity in his eyes. "Even if I don't want Platirius to have another king?"

"I'll take you over Platirius. In my eyes, you *are* Platirius. We're committed to each other. That's enough for me."

"Thank you, Asa."

"For what?"

"For loving me at my worst."

"That's easy to do. I hope to win the respect of your daughters too."

"I'd love that. I think Teenah and Tyre approve of us already, but it might take a while with Tarah. It's been hard for her to let go of her father."

"And what about her mother? Is she free of General Kron?"

She ran her hand over his chiseled abs. "Yes, when I said goodbye to Lucian, I meant it. He was my first love, but it's not fair to him or to me to hold on to the past. I know he's resting well."

"Good. Are you hungry?"

She nodded. "Very."

"What would you like?"

"Hmmm. Hazelnut-toffee-butter cookies!"

"Just cookies?" he asked.

"I love them!" she declared.

"And I love you," he said, staring into her eyes. "Does that scare you?

"A little, but I'm not fighting it anymore. I was afraid to admit it before, but I feel so good when I'm with you."

Their kiss was sweeter than any dessert she'd ever consumed.

"I'll make sure you always do. Now? Food. I don't think cookies will do it for me. Let's add some sandwiches."

As he entered an order into the TranScreen, Queen Vivant lay on his chest, ready to embrace whatever blessings the universe sent her way.

"**K**nock, knock," said King Justin.

Fawn looked up from her TranScreen and removed her glasses. "We've been over this, Your Highness. I'm grateful to you for performing my surgery, but you don't work here anymore."

He raised his hands in mock surrender. "I know. I just came to see how you're doing."

Hearing her laugh made everything right in his world. "I'm fine! Have you spoken with General Lyric?"

He shook his head. "Nope. I have no reason to."

Quietly, she observed his pensive expression.

"I realized there was always something between Lyric and I. Her career, then her mother. Now that she's out of her life, she has her career back, and she's happier than I've ever seen her. I'll never be number one in her life, and that's just not good enough for me anymore. Does that make sense?"

She nodded. "Yes. Honestly, I can see both sides. I worked hard to get where I am too. For generations, WomenForms have been denied the chance to have careers. It's very important to be able to stand on your own without a MaleForm's assistance...or permission."

"Ah! Let's say there's a king whom you knew before he became a king."

Amused, she sat back and crossed her arms over her chest. "Yes?"

"And the two of you struck up a friendship that slowly turned into something more on his part. What if...this king asked you to be his queen?"

"I'd say even if I had deep feelings for my friend, it would bother me if I had to give up my career. I'd become very depressed if I couldn't be a doctor anymore."

He nodded, tapping his fingers on her desk. "Fair enough. What if the king wanted his queen to continue saving lives after they married? Would that make her happy?"

The warm glow in her eyes set his heart to racing. "I'd say that would make her very happy, My King."

D.L.'s Note

Dear Reader,

Congratulations! You're trip to JanIus has finally come to an end! I truly hoped you enjoyed reading about Prince Justin's exciting new journey. Consequently, I'm very interested in hearing what you liked best.

Feel free to leave a review and let me know what you think. What can I say about my beloved JanIus series? Am I sad it's over? Yes and no. Although it's difficult to say goodbye to my characters, the magic begins when they're discovered by wonderful people like you.

I have an exciting new world that I can't wait to introduce to you—Maieman! That's right. Very soon, you'll learn all about General Kron's family. The new storyline will be centered around King Jonah.

I'm having a blast writing it! I hope you'll be equally as excited as I am while I take these amazing characters as far as they can go.

Well, Reader, I'd love to stay and chat, but I have books to write. Thank you for rocking with me. Please take care and stay true to yourself!

Until next time,

xoxo D.L.

Author's Bio

D.L. Hannah was born in Youngstown, Ohio. She is a writer, entrepreneur, and host of the Amerisogyny podcast. She is a Psi Chi and Alpha Kappa Delta member and earned a Bachelor of Arts degree in Clinical Community Psychology from Walsh University. For over twenty years, she has been a strong advocate for children diagnosed with Autism. She now lives in North Carolina with her family.

Join my VIP list

Join my VIP at www.dlhannah.com

Also by D.L. Hannah